Dear God, I Don't Get It

Patti Maguire Armstrong

ILLUSTRATED BY SHANNON WIRRENGA

Liguori
LIGUORI, MISSOURI

Imprimi Potest:
Harry Grile, CSsR, Provincial
Denver Province, The Redemptorists

Published by Liguori Publications
Liguori, Missouri 63057

To order, call 800-325-9521
www.liguori.org

Library of Congress Cataloging-in-Publication Data

Armstrong, Patti Maguire.
Dear God, I don't get it / Patti Maguire Armstrong; illustrated by Shannon Wirrenga. — First edition.
pages cm
Originally published by Bezalel Books, 2009.
I. Wirrenga, Shannon, illustrator. II. Title. III. Title: Dear God, I do not get it.
PZ7.A73378De 2013
[Fic]—dc23
2013002321

pISBN: 978-0-7648-2246-9
eISBN: 978-0-7648-6799-6

Liguori Publications, a nonprofit corporation, is an apostolate of The Redemptorists. To learn more about The Redemptorists, visit Redemptorists.com.

Printed in the United States of America
17 16 15 14 13 / 5 4 3 2 1
First Edition

For fun stories, games, and more...
visit DearGodBooks.com

To find news about the series...
visit Dear God Books on Facebook
or Liguori.org

Contents

Chapter 1

Bad News

There was a time in my life when I felt that bad things happened to other people but not to me. I'm not talking about everyday stuff like a bike crash or losing things, but the kinds of things that change your life.

It sounds kind of silly now, but I used to think that as long as I prayed and asked God to watch over me, I didn't need to worry about the big things. When something bad did actually happen to our family, it was such a shock that I felt like God had let me down.

I had just walked into the house after playing basketball with my best friend, Jesse Miller. We were both twelve and in the sixth grade. Our friendship began on the first day of kindergarten when we were the only two kids who cried when our moms left. The teacher had us sit together. She probably figured we would understand each other, but some other kids might think we were babies for crying. We were best friends from that day on.

The conversation I overheard in the kitchen threatened to change all that. "What are we going to do?" Mom asked Dad. Mom had a way of acting like she was staying calm, but the high tone of her voice said otherwise.

"Anne, somehow we'll manage. I can get unemployment for a few months. I hope to find another job soon." Whenever Mom's voice became strained, Dad talked slower. "I talked to a realtor about putting the house on the market. We need to be realistic and be prepared to move. There's only two other radio stations in town, and neither one has an opening."

I had heard enough. "What?" I yelled. "We can't move! Dad, there has to be a job for you somewhere. All my friends are here!" My whole life was in Kalispell, Montana.

Right then, my nine-year-old brother, Luke, came into the kitchen. As usual, the very thing that upset me made him happy. "We're going to move? Let's move near the ocean!"

This is a good time to tell you about us, the Ajax family. My dad, Paul, is tall and has dark-brown hair and a beard. He works as a radio news broadcaster. I grew up hearing him on the radio. I have always enjoyed people asking me, "Is that your dad on the radio?" I also like having my dad coach my baseball and basketball teams, although I'm not so crazy about him as a spectator. He acts like he's still the coach—only from the bleachers. I can always hear his voice above the whole crowd.

My mom, Anne, writes magazine articles, loves animals, and lets us have lots of pets. Mom is easygoing about most things except cleaning our room. She is on the short side and has medium-length brown hair, which she usually wears in a ponytail.

I think my brother Luke loves having me as an older brother so he can bug me. He has a way of making me feel like I'm missing out on something or like he knows something I don't. Mom says it's his hobby and to just ignore it. But how can I ignore pig noises at night when I'm trying to sleep or his telling my friends that he saw me playing with dolls? (I was just carrying them home for a friend.)

Luke is in third grade and has blond hair. (He likes to ask, "Why did I get the golden hair and Aaron's is mud-colored?") Luke collects bugs, both living and dead (which I hate), and loves anything to do with nature. When we aren't fighting, we are best friends. I guess it's a brother thing.

My youngest brother is Tyler. He is four years old and is the best. He looks up to me and is always ready for a hug. Even if I'm in trouble with Mom or Dad or if Luke and I are fighting, I can always count on my little buddy. Tyler has dark-brown hair. He doesn't always speak correctly, so he calls me Air-yun instead of Aaron. This is much better than what Luke called me at that age—Air-yuck.

As for me, I'm average height for twelve, and my hair is brown—not muddy but sorta milk-chocolate colored. I have a few freckles and a small scar at the side of my right eyebrow. The scar is a souvenir from when I was four and tried to fly by jumping out of a tree. On my way down, I tangled with a branch. I'm average in sports but above average in school—especially in math, my favorite subject.

There is also our mutt from the animal shelter. We named her Waggles because when she greets us, her whole body wags along with her tail. Waggles looks a lot like a collie but with something else mixed in. We have no idea what that "something else" might be. Luke claims he knows, but only so that when I ask him, he can say, "I'm not going to tell you."

Our cat, Gumdrop, is black and white and usually sleeps at the foot of my bed when she's not walking around at night. In addition to turtles, frogs, toads, newts, salamanders, and fish that come and go regularly at our house, we have a blue parakeet named Leonardo and a white rabbit named Cotton.

I should also tell you that shortly before this time, things had changed in our family concerning God. It used to be that if we had friends over or if we went camping, we might not go to church on Sunday. We usually said grace before meals and bedtime prayers, but that was it. A few months before my dad lost his job, we began saying morning prayers and reading the Bible and stories about the saints. We also stopped missing church on Sundays. My mom and dad told us they realized that if God was supposed to be the most important thing in our lives, then we should act like it.

But hearing about my dad losing his job confused things. We had been paying more attention to God, so why wasn't God taking better care of us? The radio station where Dad worked was making less money, so they needed to lay off one of their reporters. The other reporter had worked there for twenty years, so my dad was let go.

There weren't any other job openings in radio or even at the newspaper or the two TV stations where we lived. He also tried to find a job where he could be some kind of manager, but there wasn't anything.

The fact that Kalispell is a small town in the valley of the Rocky Mountain range near Glacier Park makes it an amazing place to live. But it also means that jobs don't open up very often, and when they do, people are always lined up to fill them. It ended up that we had to move, which meant that God had not answered my prayers. I even promised not to fight with Luke anymore and to keep my room clean, but nothing worked. My parents taught us that God loves us even more than we love ourselves. Well, I love myself enough that I want to be happy; instead, I was miserable.

God made the whole universe, so I knew he could find my dad a job if he wanted. So even worse than leaving Kalispell was the feeling that God really didn't care about me. This was something I did not admit to my parents. I prayed with the family during family prayers, but at that point, my lips were moving but not my heart.

Chapter 2

Moving Day

My dad had taken a radio job in Bismarck, North Dakota. In Montana, people tell North Dakotan jokes. I even told a few.

Moving was bad enough, but why did it have to be to North Dakota? I asked my parents if I could keep my Montana citizenship, but they laughed. I guess citizenship only applies to countries, not states.

I thought Luke and I did a great job packing up our stuff, but Mom disagreed. "Aaron, we don't need to bring a bag of cow bones with us," she said.

"I was hoping to get a cow skull and try to put together a whole skeleton," I said.

"Sorry, there isn't enough room for that." She opened up another big bag. "And we are definitely not moving all these rusty cans."

"But, Mom," I said, "those are like antiques and might be valuable someday. They rusted because they were made with steel. Today, cans are aluminum."

We also had to give away all our animals except Waggles and Gumdrop. The frogs, toads, and one turtle were returned to the pond where we found them. Tyler slipped on one of the frogs when Luke dumped out the bucket. I think it will be all right, but he hops with a little limp now.

It was hard to give our parakeet, Leonardo, away. I had just taught him to say "pretty bird" and "good morning." He had taught himself to say, "It wasn't me." I guess he'd heard it enough around our house that he'd picked it up on his own.

Cotton, our rabbit, was given to family friends with two girls. Before I was even done explaining how to take care of Cotton, they had put him in a pink dress. I told them he was a boy, but that didn't matter. Poor Cotton.

I said goodbye to Jesse the night before at a farewell sleepover he had in my honor. Our whole group was there: Sid Peters, Clay Jenson, Carter Wilson, and Chet Bender. I had no appetite when we sat around the table for pizza, but I took small bites so I wasn't just sitting and doing nothing. Each bite was hard to swallow.

"It's weird that after tonight, we might not see you ever again," Chet said.

"Yeah, weird," I replied.

"Instead of six of us, there will just be five," Clay added.

"Hey," Sid said, "that means we'll have uneven teams at recess."

Jesse looked like I felt—trying to act like everything was OK, but he knew it wasn't. "It won't seem right on Monday when you don't stop by to get me for school," he said.

"But don't worry," Carter said, "I'll think of you every time I look up at the cracked clock in the gym and remember the ball you kicked so hard during gym class."

"I'll think of you during lunch," Sid said. "Remember when you brought a raw egg? Was that really an accident?"

"Sid, do you have any idea how sticky and gross my clothes were the rest of the day? Paper towels couldn't get it all off."

When the lights went out and things quieted down around 1:00 AM, I couldn't get to sleep. I knew that when I left Jesse's house the next morning, I would not be coming back. Jesse would miss me, but he'd still have the other guys. I'd be an outsider.

When I finally started getting sleepy, I remembered I hadn't said my prayers. I always said nighttime prayers with my family or on my own if I was away. That's when I realized I felt like an outsider with God too. If God had answered my prayers, I would not be having a terrible time at my farewell party. I started praying the Our Father out of habit, but then I drifted off to sleep.

In the morning, Jesse and I acted like we hardly knew each other. We didn't know how to say goodbye. I couldn't get all mushy and tell him how much I was going to miss him. Just then, Jesse's mom came to the rescue.

"It seems like just yesterday that you two became friends." Jesse and I nodded as she continued. "You two used to swing for hours in our backyard. Remember how you'd jump off and have contests of who could go the highest? We're sure going to miss you around here, but you and Jesse will always be friends. Real friendships never end."

Then she put out her arms and said, "Hey, group hug, everyone!" Jesse and I promised to call each other, and our parents said we could set up e-mail accounts to keep in touch. I was going to miss Jesse, but it was a relief to leave his house. Saying goodbye was hard. I was glad to get it over with.

Back at my house—which wasn't my home anymore—the move was in progress. Watching the movers take furniture and boxes out, my insides hollowed out along with the house. Luke skipped upstairs and down, watching the activity. Tyler held Snoopy, his stuffed dog with floppy ears, under his arm and followed behind Luke. For them, it was a big adventure.

"Want to take one last look at the house before we leave?" Dad asked, coming up behind me and putting his arm around my shoulder.

"Nah," I answered. "What's the point?" I wanted to remember the house like it was when we lived in it, not like a skeleton waiting for another family to make it a home again.

"I'll just wait in the van," I said. I grabbed my backpack and got into my favorite seat in the very back next to a window. Luke would want the middle seat by the window on the driver's side, right in front of me. That way, we could play games or talk, or Luke could have fun bugging me. Tyler usually switched back and forth between Luke's seat and mine on long trips. Waggles would do the same, and Gumdrop traveled in a small kennel.

It was an unseasonably warm Saturday in February, but still, I began to feel cold just sitting in the van. I got out and walked around the house. The afternoon sun melted icicles on the trees. I looked over at the tree responsible for my scar when I had practiced flying. Its long, arching branches dripped big drops onto the sidewalk. It was as if it were crying. I swallowed hard and wondered why a person's throat always swelled up when he was trying not to cry.

I focused on the mountain peaks I could see between the houses and the treetops. We had gone on many hikes on some of those mountains. Our family often got together with other families to camp and ride bikes in Glacier National Park. There were wild animals in those mountains. We had seen moose, mountain goats, and bears a few times. Now all the wildness and adventure in those rocky peaks would be left behind for the plains of North Dakota.

Finally, the rest of the family came out of the house. A few of the neighbors came out to say goodbye. People were hugging and crying, so I hurried into the van to avoid it. After everyone had piled in and buckled up, Dad shouted, "Goodbye, everyone. Come visit us in Bismarck." We waved as our van pulled away. Tyler was still waving after our house and neighbors were no longer in sight.

"They're gone, Tyler." I said. "You can stop now."

"I don't want the goodbye to end, Air-yun," he answered.

"Well, it's over," I said. "The best part of our lives is behind us now."

Mom turned around in her seat. "Aaron," she said, "I know this is hard for you, but you have years to make new friends and memories in our new home."

"Think positive," Dad added. "We prayed, and God has led us to North Dakota. As a matter of fact," he said, "let's start our trip with a prayer. Dear Lord, thank you for all that you've given to us, for my new job, and for one another. We pray for your guidance and ask you to keep us safe and close to you during our trip to North Dakota."

I couldn't concentrate very well, but hearing the words felt right for some reason. I was tired of feeling angry at God. I hadn't actually admitted to myself that I was angry at him, but that's what it was. I knew that since God had made us, he must love us too. My head told me God still cared about me, but my heart still felt empty and let down.

"Dear God," I prayed, "I don't get it. I don't understand why you want to take us from Montana to North Dakota. It seems like my parents are trying to do everything you want them to do, but still we have to move. I don't get it. Help me accept whatever lies ahead." I closed my eyes. They were heavy from the lack of sleep at the sleepover the night before, and I soon drifted off.

Chapter 3

On the Road

I opened my eyes and saw a lady in the car next to me blowing her nose. *What am I doing with my face smashed against the car window?* It took only seconds for me to remember the awful truth—we were leaving Montana and headed to a place I had thus far only heard about in jokes.

If North Dakotans did only a fraction of the things talked about in jokes, life was going to get ugly. Then a terrible thought occurred to me—we would be a whole family of North Dakotans! Not only would I be a North Dakotan but a friendless one. I would be the dreaded "new kid" at school.

I thought back to fourth grade when Willy Delmore was the new kid at school. At first, Jessie and I thought he was strange because he wore red pants on his first day. But after he passed out gummy worms on the playground and it turned out he could run faster than all the other boys, we forgot about the pants. Anyway, his mom must have bought them on sale and made him wear them.

In sixth grade, I knew bringing gummy worms was not going to be the way to make friends, and I was only an average runner. To top it off, when I first got to know people, my shyness caused me to blush easily. Then it never failed that someone would shout out, "Your face is turning red!" As if I *needed* to be told.

Thinking about it all just upset my stomach. I focused my attention on what Luke was doing. He and Tyler were toward the end of a car-bingo game.

"Mind if I play?" I asked.

"In a few minutes," Luke said. "All I need is a cow to win. Tyler still needs a police car and a department store. We'll be on the highway for hours, so there's not much hope for him to spot a store."

Tyler laughed. "Ha, ha, I found a store!" he said, pointing to a sign along the highway.

"No way!" Luke said. "That's a sign, not a store."

Dad stepped in and sided with Tyler. "There is a store at the bottom of that sign, you just can't see it from the highway. It seems only fair that Tyler should get to count it."

"Ha, ha! I win, I win!" Tyler yelled.

"No, you don't," Luke said. "You still need to find a police car."

"I did win!" he said. "There's one!" Sure enough, lights flashed behind us. My dad pulled over to the shoulder of the road and rolled down his window.

"Sir," the policeman said with a grin on his face, "are you aware you have a rope hanging out of your car with a stuffed animal on the end of it?"

"What?" Dad asked.

"That's Snoopy!" said Tyler. "He's my doggy. He's walking outside."

Tyler often tied a rope around Snoopy's neck and pretended to take him for a walk. No one had noticed at the last rest area that Tyler had kept Snoopy outside the car. It was a thin rope, and the car door had closed on it.

When the officer brought Snoopy to the car, Tyler burst into tears. The fur on Snoopy's back end was worn off from bouncing against the pavement.

"Don't cry," Mom said. "I'll make Snoopy a pair of pants once we get settled." Tyler wiped his eyes and snuggled his face into his scraped-up stuffed dog. Dad thanked the officer, and we got back on the highway.

Luke, Tyler, and I played a couple more games of car bingo before getting bored. I looked through my backpack to find something else to do. Each of us had filled backpacks for the trip. Dad had taken us to a store where we picked out a few things, like cards, games, Silly Putty, and a couple of treats. I pulled out a book and a box of chocolate-covered nuts. Tyler and Luke noticed and pulled out their boxes of candy.

I put my hand into my box and quickly pulled it out. "Gross! Who did this? Luke, you must have done this!"

Everyone turned to look at me. "Aaron, your yelling almost caused me to run off the road," Dad said.

Luke and Tyler stared wide-eyed. "What's wrong?" Mom asked.

"Someone has slimed my chocolate-covered peanuts!" I said. "They're all slippery and gross. And I have a pretty good idea just who it was," I said, sticking my face into Luke's.

Luke moved the mouthful of caramels he was working on into his right cheek. "It wasn't me," he said. "I was planning on trading some of my candy for yours, but not anymore."

"Oh, then I suppose Waggles licked my candy," I said sarcastically.

Big tears streamed down Tyler's face. "Air-yun," he cried. "I was just tasting some. I put them all back, honest. You can have my candy."

I looked at him holding out a piece of his slobbery licorice. "No, that's OK. I'm not really even hungry, but thanks anyway." Dad thanked me for understanding and added that we would stop soon at a restaurant for dinner.

After another uneventful hour on the road, Dad turned off the highway and found a Beefy Boy restaurant—my favorite. Even though I was getting older, I still loved to push the button on the talking cow in front of every Beefy Boy. Tyler ran ahead to be the first one to push it.

"Try our new milk-chocolate smoo-moothies," the cow said. He pushed it again, and the cow mooed a couple times then said, "Don't let your milk give you a moo-stache. Buy one of my plastic cow straws inside."

I gently moved Tyler aside and pushed the button myself. A terrible screeching sound came out of the speaker under the cow. I pushed it again, but the screeching sound only got worse.

"Air-yun broke the cow!" Tyler cried. "Mom, Dad, he broke it!"

"All I did was push the button," I said.

"Don't worry about it," Dad said. "We'll tell the manager inside that his cow isn't working."

As we walked into the restaurant, Luke announced in a loud voice, "My big brother just broke your cow outside. There's going to be a lot of disappointed kids now." My dad quickly explained that I had only pressed the button. He then told Luke that if he wanted his help in the future, he would ask for it.

Luke, Tyler, and I all ordered hamburgers, fries, and chocolate smoothies. When our food came, we said grace and ate. Mom and Dad talked about mostly boring things, like how many miles to a gallon of gas we were getting and when the moving van would arrive.

The plan was for us to stay in a hotel until we found a house to buy. My parents were worried how long that might take. I didn't want to think about it. A new house, a new school, a new town—it all made my head spin and stomach swirl.

"Aren't you going to eat your fries, Aaron?" Luke asked.

"I'll sell them to you," I offered.

"No, thanks," he answered. "But you know how Mom and Dad feel about wasting food."

I pushed my plate over to him. "No charge—this time."

"Well, looks like we're ready to hit the road again," Dad said. We got back into the car and continued driving into our future, into the darkness of night. It seemed so fitting.

Chapter 4

Overnight

We drove for a few hours before stopping at a motel. "Dozey Doze Inn," announced a neon red-and-white sign above a bare yellow building. An empty swimming pool lay between the motel and highway. Other than a gas station with an attached convenience store, there was nothing else as far as the eye could see. A whistling wind collected a dusting of snow into small, moving drifts. I imagined that even in the summer, the place probably lacked warmth. Under the flashing sign hung another one that read, "Children and Pets Welcome—Reasonable Rates."

We held our overnight bags in front of our bodies to block the wind and hurried inside. Our room looked as exciting as the outside of the building did—two queen-sized beds with orange bedspreads, a TV, a table, a dresser, orange carpeting, and a bathroom. Oh, and two different pictures of fruit bowls on the wall.

It was my job to get the cat out of the car and set up her litter box next to the bathroom. Dad took Waggles for a walk. Both animals were hyper. Gumdrop kept pouncing on my feet as if they were a mouse.

Tyler snacked on crackers, and Luke jumped into a hot bath. Since I had started taking showers, baths seemed babyish, but that night, it felt like a good idea.

"Hurry up, Luke, so I have time to take one," I said.

"I'll see what I can do," he said. "It's going to take a while."

I looked into the tub. A dozen plastic army figures from his backpack were floating in individual styrofoam cups.

"Luke, when are you going to grow up? And what are we supposed to drink out of now that you turned our cups into boats?"

"These are from the front desk. I took them when Dad checked in," he said. "And I am growing up. I just know how to enjoy myself while I'm doing it."

"You stole those cups."

"Did not. The sign said, 'For our customers.'"

"That's for people who want to drink coffee, not for bath toys. You stole," I said.

"Mom, Aaron is accusing me of doing something I didn't do."

I explained the situation to Mom. "Luke, the cups were really not meant to be used as bath toys, so don't do something like that again." She looked at me. "He wasn't stealing when he took the cups because he thought it was all right."

Figures. Luke is the only guy I know who can sin without sinning.

I finally got Luke kicked out of the tub when the waves he made for his "storm at sea" sloshed onto the floor.

Once everyone had bathed, we watched a *Lost in Space* episode, an old TV rerun. I failed to convince my parents to let us watch *Godzilla vs. King Kong.* Mom said it would give Tyler nightmares. Dad said he was glad we didn't get cable at home. When I reminded him that we were actually homeless now, he either didn't hear me or he chose to ignore my comment.

Dad wanted to get an early start the next day, so TV was turned off. We said our usual evening prayers. After saying some regular prayers, we all take turns saying one of our own. I thought for a moment and then finally prayed, "Dear God, thank you for our family. Please help all babies to be born into loving families, and, and, ummm...please help me feel better about moving and accept your plan for our family."

Out of the corner of my eye I saw Mom and Dad look at each other and smile. I hate it when they do that. After we closed with, "In the name of the Father and of the Son and of the Holy Spirit," Luke stood up and grabbed the sleeping bag.

"Someone has to sleep on the floor, and I call it first," he said.

"No fair!" I said. "I want to sleep on the floor." I actually hadn't even thought about it but automatically argued against Luke getting first choice. Tyler wanted his stuffed dog to sleep on something soft after the rough ride outside the car, so he stayed out of it. Mom said we should flip a coin. I called heads and won. But after the lights went out and I lay on the hard orange floor, I wondered if I had actually won.

That Luke, I thought, *even when he loses, it seems like he wins.* I tossed and turned for what seemed like an hour, then I finally sat up. Dad was snoring, and everyone else seemed to be asleep too. If I didn't get some sleep, I'd *really* be crabby in the morning. I couldn't get comfortable on the thin, orange carpet, which I now realized smelled like peanuts. *Why hadn't I just let Luke have the floor like he wanted?*

My mom always says, "Where there's a will, there's a way," so I decided to put that saying into practice. I thought about carefully sliding Luke's sleeping body onto the floor, but he'd probably wake up or I might drop him. I could wake him and ask if he wanted to change places, but that seemed doomed to fail. He would suspect there was something fishy about my sudden offer.

Then an idea hit me. I wouldn't have to ask Luke to trade places with me if he didn't *want* to sleep in the bed. If there were creepy, crawly things running across his feet and nibbling at his toes, he just might beg me for my spot on the floor.

I slowly lifted the blanket and sheet at the foot of the bed and slipped my arm under. Using two fingers, I imagined a big black beetle and pitter-pattered

my fingers lightly across Luke's foot. I did this a few times. All he did was curl his legs up further under the blanket. I crawled up under the blanket to reach his feet. Taking a deep breath, I began again. The pitter-pattering was a little heavier this time so he would notice it.

It was getting hot and stuffy under the blanket. I hadn't realized Luke could be such a deep sleeper. My two fingers did a heavier pitter-patter from his foot up to his knee. I made slight squeaking noises and then pinched his knees with my fingernails so he would think something bit him. Just as I was pinching, I realized I'd better quickly slip out from under the blanket before I was discovered.

Suddenly, a large thud with claws landed on my back. Gumdrop shrieked and bit me through the blanket. I screamed, "That hurt!" Waggles pounced on the bed and barked wildly.

Luke *finally* woke up and yelled out, "Danger, danger. Alien alert!" (He must have been dreaming about the *Lost in Space* episode.) Tyler screamed and started crying. My dad turned on the light and yelled, "What is going on here?"

My mom noticed me gone. "Aaron is gone!" she screamed. I was tangled up in the blanket and sheet by now and couldn't get out right away. It took several more minutes before all the screaming, barking, and meowing settled down—but not soon enough, however. There was a knock at our door. Dad jumped up to open it. A man in a blue jacket with the words

"Dozey Doze Motel" in white lettering surveyed the room. He eyed us one by one.

"What's going on in here?" he asked. "This is a nice, quiet family motel. I've worked here for seven years, but I've never heard the kind of screaming and carrying on that I just heard coming from your room. You are either going to have to quiet down or I will ask you to leave."

My parents apologized and promised there would be no more noise from our room. "Well, there had better not be," he said and walked out. The room became quiet—completely silent. All eyes were on me.

I explained, but no one looked either sympathetic or amused. When I finished, Dad asked Luke, "Do you want to trade places with him?" To my complete shock, he said yes. He could have left me on the floor, knowing I'd be miserable. That's when it occurred to me that even though Luke took pleasure in annoying me sometimes, he really was never mean. Come to think of it, he wasn't one to even get revenge at me for the times I was not so nice to him. Most of his pestering was usually caused accidentally or by his annoying sense of humor.

The room became quiet as everyone settled into their spots. Then everyone—including me—got to sleep.

Chapter 5

New Home

The rest of the drive to Bismarck was pretty uneventful. We played games, listened to music—all the usual car things. Every now and then I got an empty feeling in my stomach. The longer we drove, the further away my life in Kalispell became. When we crossed the Memorial Bridge into Bismarck, the pit in my stomach opened up into a big black hole. Entering Bismarck made everything real.

"We're here!" Dad shouted, tooting the horn as we crossed the bridge. I looked down on the frozen Missouri River framed with lifeless brown trees. At least in the western part of Montana, the white-capped mountains and evergreen forests keep everything looking like a postcard even in the dead of winter.

Our first stop was another motel. This place was a little nicer. It was called the Carriage House and was located right in town. I thought we should go check out the mall that was nearby, but my parents insisted on business before pleasure—which meant house hunting. For the next two days we must have looked at every house for sale in all of Bismarck.

Looking at houses got old quickly. I felt like I was trespassing. People's pictures hung on the wall, and all their stuff was in their house. One older home had an attic with so much old junk that a person could spend months exploring it all. The owner was elderly and had moved to California, so the real-estate agent said the house was being sold "as is"—junk and all. Luke and I wanted the house based on the attic alone, but my parents were not impressed. Then there was the house with a built-in pool in the yard. Too dangerous and too much work, Dad said. If the kitchen was too small, Mom disliked it right away.

The more we looked, the more I missed our house in Kalispell. Then at the end of the second day, we found a house everyone liked. It was a blue and white ninety-year-old three-story house with a fireplace. It had five bedrooms and a spooky unfinished basement with thick granite walls. The big front porch had a porch swing. It was in the older section of town and within walking distance to things like the library, the post office, and a plaza with a few stores.

The house was vacant, and the owners were willing to let us move in right away. We could rent it while my parents worked with a bank to get all the paperwork done to buy it. Everyone was so excited about the big old house that we slept in sleeping bags the next night since it would be another day before our moving truck arrived. The truck was waiting in Montana until we had found a place to move into.

Spending the night in a big, empty house was almost

like camping. My dad played hide-and-seek with us. With all the closets, attics, and rooms on three floors plus the basement, it took a while before everyone was found, though no one actually dared to hide in the basement. Tyler was always easy to find because he giggled whenever he heard footsteps approaching.

We sat on the floor and ate pizza in front of a fire in the fireplace. At bedtime we all gathered in the room that would be my parents' bedroom and said our prayers. We laid out sleeping bags, and everyone slept together on the floor. Even Waggles and Gumdrop slept with us. They seemed pretty confused about all the moving and wouldn't let us out of their sight. Tyler cuddled up between Luke and me, and the animals curled up at our feet. It was such a fun and cozy night with my family in the comfort of our new home.

The next morning was Saturday. By 10:00 AM, the movers arrived. Mom assigned Luke to help her unpack dishes in the kitchen while I was put in charge of keeping Tyler out of trouble. It was a good time to get a look at the neighborhood. It wasn't too cold—in the thirties—so I put a leash on Waggles and dressed Tyler warmly.

Our house sat on a corner, with an alley in back. We walked to the end of the block through the alley, looking at backyards as we went. Only one had a tree fort, and another had a pile of sleds behind its garage. Otherwise, I couldn't tell if there were many kids in the neighborhood.

At the end of the block and across the street was the real reason I had ventured out—Will-Moore School. It was a wide, yellow-brick building. My old school was red brick.

"Come on, Tyler," I said, taking his mittened hand. "Let's walk around the school. There's probably a playground in the back."

Sure enough, we discovered a huge, brightly-colored playground on the other side. There were long, rect-angular bars with a handle in the center that allowed you to push off and glide from one end to the other. Twisty slides, tire swings, a moving bridge between two sets of spider-web monkey bars—all kinds of things.

"Air-yun," Tyler yelled, "we must be in wonderland!" He ran laughing and squealing to one of the slides. For the next hour we had the playground to ourselves.

Then, like reality often does, it hit—hard. Reality was in the form of a snowball right smack on the side of my head. I turned and saw a girl around my age, with short brown hair and freckles. Then I realized in horror that we were both wearing the same jackets—blue with a silver stripe around the chest and sleeves. How embarrassing!

"What's your problem?" I asked.

"It looks like you are," the girl said. "Why don't you go play at your own school?"

"I hate to break this to you, but this is my own school," I said. "Or at least it will be. I just moved here from Montana." It occurred to me that it would be a good idea to make peace rather than starting school with an enemy. "I'm Aaron Ajax," I said, trying to sound friendly. "What's your name?"

The angry look remained on her face. "My mom taught me not to talk to strangers, and you look pretty strange." Just then, Tyler began pelting her with snowballs. "Hey, get your little midget under control!" she yelled and walked off.

"I took care of her for you, Air-yun," Tyler announced happily, his pink-cheeked face peeking out of a big, puffy hood.

"You're a good brother, Tyler, but I was trying to get along with her," I said, then added, "Of course, I wasn't doing very well."

"Oops," Tyler said. "Sorry, Air-yun. I was trying to help."

"It's all right," I said. "I think we've had enough fresh air and snowballs for now. Let's get back home." I took Tyler's mittened hand as we headed back.

"Air-yun," Tyler began as we trudged along, "do you like our new house?"

"Yes," I answered truthfully. "It's the rest I'm worried about." I realized life was so simple at his age. He was too young to understand what I was up against.

"I love our house," Tyler said. "I'm glad God moved us, just like I prayed for."

"What?" I cried, stopping in my tracks. "You mean the whole time I was asking God to let us stay in Kalispell, you were praying we would move?"

Tyler laughed. "Yep. God liked my prayers better."

I walked in silence the rest of the way home. I had never thought about such a situation. How does God handle it when two people are praying for the exact opposite? Did God say "yes" to Tyler's prayers and "no" to mine because he was more deserving? Did Tyler pray harder than I did?

I felt better saying my prayers and talking to God than not doing so, but now that my prayers hadn't been answered in the way I'd hoped, I wondered what the point was of praying at all. And how could prayers matter when two people prayed for opposite things? I had no answers, so I brushed the thoughts away as we walked back inside the house.

Chapter 6

Neighborhood

Even though we had unpacked boxes all day and night on Saturday, we had plenty more. The furniture was mostly in place. Dad had put up our beds, and most of our clothes were either in closets or dressers. Since it was Sunday, we would take a break for a while and go to church.

Bismarck had five Catholic churches and we were going to Mass at the one closest to our house, Church of the Holy Spirit. After Dad took his shower, he began (as usual) announcing in five-minute intervals how many minutes were left before departure. "Thirty minutes! Thirty minutes, and we're leaving!" Then it was, "Twenty-five minutes remaining!"

By the time Dad began his "Ten minutes and I'm out of here" announcement, Tyler ran through the house screaming that he couldn't find Snoopy. Mom told me to hurry and put on a nicer shirt, and she told Luke to go wash the food off his face. Then Dad announced he was leaving with or without us and headed for the car. The rest of us ran around for another minute and then hurried out the door, with the exception of Mom, who ran back to turn off all the lights and put Waggles in the yard.

Church of the Holy Spirit was about ten blocks away. My parents usually sat near the front because they said we paid attention better, but most of the front seats were already taken. It felt odd to be in a church full of strangers. There were no friends to wave to or talk with after Mass. The church was much bigger than our church in Kalispell. The ceilings were a couple stories high. A large crucifix hung over an immense white marble altar. To the right was a side altar with a statue of the Blessed Mother holding Baby Jesus. I missed our old church.

The Mass in Bismarck was the same as the one we attended in Kalispell. Because we are "one" Church, no matter where in the world we go to Mass, it's basically the same. During Mass, I asked God to help me have faith in him. My mind wandered a lot, but when I noticed, I'd try and pay attention to what was going on.

After Mass, there was coffee and juice and muffins in the church basement. My parents were meeting new people, and Luke met two boys his age. I sat with Tyler and kept going back for more muffins rather than just sit there doing nothing. On the way home, my parents talked about what a nice parish Church of the Holy Spirit seemed to be. Luke told everyone about his new friends, Mac and Quinn. They were in the same grade at Will-Moore school, and they said he could sit at their lunch table on Monday. Tyler just sucked his thumb and hugged Snoopy. I looked out the window, feeling a bit sick from all the muffins I ate. The taste of the last blueberry one (number four, I think) left a bad taste in my mouth.

"Looks like we have a visitor," Dad said, pulling into our driveway. Knocking at the door to our house was a small, gray-haired lady holding something in her hands. "Helloooo, neighbors!" the lady said in a high, soft voice, walking toward our car. "I'm Adele Murples, and I live right next-door. I brought over a chocolate cake to welcome you to the neighborhood."

"Oh, how nice," Mom said. She introduced our family, and then added, "Our house is still a shambles, but you're welcome to come in for a cup of coffee." The adults and Tyler went into the house.

As they all went inside, Luke and I noticed two boys on the other side of the house from across the alley walk up to the fence and start petting Waggles.

We approached them slowly.

"Hi," I said. "Do you guys live around here?"

"Yeah," said the big kid. He had sandy-brown hair and stood about a head taller than me. The other boy looked almost like his twin, only he stood a head shorter than me. Both kids were husky, with rounded faces.

"I'm Josh, and this is my brother," the big kid said. "His real name is Wesley, but everyone calls him Buster. What grade are you guys in?"

It turned out that Josh was in my grade and Buster was in Luke's. We talked about things like how many kids were in our family, what sports we liked to play, and so on. Everything was going well until Josh asked where we had been.

"We go to Mass on Sundays," I answered.

"You guys have to go to church?" he said. "That means you probably think you are better than everyone else."

"We do not."

"Well, that's not what my dad says," Josh said.

"Well, your dad doesn't know what he's talking about," I said.

It felt like acid was burning in my mouth. Or maybe that was all the muffins talking. Whatever it was, my ears burned red and I could hardly contain myself.

Josh stood there a moment with his mouth open, then said, "I'm not going to listen to some smart-mouth insult my dad!"

"I didn't insult your dad," I said. "Your dad insulted us."

"Maybe you should move back to Montana," Josh said. "Come on, Buster, let's go." Josh stormed off, but Buster ignored him. He and Luke were busy playing fetch in the yard with Waggles by now.

I watched Josh walk off. Anger still filled me, but then a wave of sadness also washed over me. *Wow,* I thought. *I have a real talent for making enemies.* I looked over at Luke playing with *another* new friend.

Now he had three friends and I had two enemies. I felt so very homesick for Kalispell and the comfort of a best friend.

I stormed into the house and flopped on the couch, listening to my parents visit with Mrs. Murples in the dining room. Everyone was making friends. When Mrs. Murples left a few minutes later, Dad asked me what was wrong.

"Nothing much, except it's not much fun not having any friends," I said.

"Why don't you give Jesse a call," Dad said. "Sometimes it helps to talk with an old friend."

"What's the point?" I said. "But maybe I will." Jesse would probably understand.

"Hey, Jesse," I said when he answered the phone. "What's up?"

"Aaron, is that you? How's it going?"

I told him about our house, and it wasn't long before I let him in on how good I was at making enemies.

"Boy, that sure stinks," he said.

Then there was a moment of silence. "Hey, what's new with you?" I asked.

"Oh, I almost forgot to tell you, Sid Peters broke his leg snowboarding yesterday."

"You're kidding! How did he do that?" I asked.

"We were snowboarding at Woodland Park on the hill near the ice rink," Jessie said. "I told Sid there were too many trees there, but you know him, he never listens. We all went with him to the top of the hill, but he went down first. Instead of looking where he was going, he turned around to look up at us and crashed right into the tree. At first he just lay on the ground and didn't move, so we thought he was just trying to scare us."

I laughed. "Yeah, that would be just like Sid to do something like that too."

Jesse continued, "Then, when he didn't move for a long time, we got scared. Carter stayed with him, and the rest of us ran down the hill to get help. Luckily there was a guy sledding with his kid nearby who ended up calling Sid's parents."

Jesse filled me in on the details and said Sid probably wouldn't have to go to school on Monday. Hearing that dreaded word *school* brought me back to reality. Tomorrow, I had to face going to a new school where I had no friends.

We talked a little while longer before I said goodbye and promised to let Jesse know how the new school was.

"Well, do you feel better?" Dad asked.

I thought for a moment. "Sorta," I said. At least I didn't feel like a total loser anymore. Talking to a friend helped me not to feel so alone.

Chapter 7

New School

Everyone, come down for breakfast," Mom yelled from the kitchen. The smell of waffles drifted upstairs. I pulled up the covers and burrowed in. It was Monday—my first day at the new school. I couldn't eat; my stomach already felt full with a big, ugly knot.

As Luke and Tyler bounded down the steps, a flood of jealousy surged through me. They had it so easy. Tyler's life was simple. He would stay home with Mom all day. Trips to the grocery store, mud puddles, and bubble baths were still a thrill for him. All he needed to be happy was his stuffed dog, Snoopy.

Luke was another story. As a third grader, he was plenty old enough to start worrying about things like meeting people and a new school, but not Luke. He didn't seem to worry about anything. Everything always fell into place for him. He had already made three friends before even starting school. Not only did I not make any new friends yet, but I already had enemies.

My dad poked his head in my room. "Hey," he said,

"if you don't get out of bed, I'll have to take you to school in your pajamas." He wasn't starting his new job until Tuesday, so he had another day to get the house settled and to register Luke and me at school.

"Ha, ha, very funny," I said. The smile left his face as he came in and sat next to me on the bed.

"I know it's tough starting a new school," Dad said. "Remember, I moved a lot as a kid."

"How did you handle changing schools so much?" I asked.

"I was the class clown and tended to get into troub... bub, bub...Boy, those waffles are going to get cold if you don't hurry," he said. Dad paused a moment, then added, "The first day is always the hardest, so once you get through today, things will get easier. It helps if you turn your troubles over to God instead of carrying the burden alone."

"That's part of my problem," I said. "I just don't get it. It seemed like you were trying to do everything God wanted you to do, but then you lost your job. We prayed you would find a new one so we could stay in Kalispell, but we still had to move. I don't see what good it does to pray."

"Oh, OK, I see," Dad said. "Well, let me put it to you this way. When Jesus was in the Garden of Gethsemane, he prayed for his Father to remove the suffering. But then he prayed, 'Father, not my will but yours be done.' In other words, he united himself with the Father and accepted his will."

Dad paused a moment like he was thinking of what

else to say. "Jesus knew it would be hard, but he also knew the suffering was happening for a reason—to save us. So, we should pray like Jesus did, for God's will to be done. And if there is suffering attached to it, then we should ask God for the strength we need. Does any of this make sense?" Dad asked.

"I guess," I said. "I'll have to think about it."

"Many times when I haven't gotten what I wanted, down the road I saw that in God's wisdom, he gave me something better."

I crawled out of bed. "Thanks, Dad," I said. We went downstairs and joined the others for breakfast. After everyone ate and dressed, we sat in the living room for morning prayers before heading off to school. Even though it was only a block away, we dressed warmly. The weather had become brutal. It was a cold, gray day with a biting wind. Dad told us to get used to it because North Dakota was known for strong winds. My cheeks stung and my nose dripped by the time we got to school.

Before we went inside, Dad hugged us and said, "I love you guys and I'll be praying that everything goes great today." We went to the principal's office to register before he took Luke to his third-grade classroom and me to my sixth-grade room. It was still early, so there were only a handful of kids walking around.

I met my new teacher, Mrs. Eppner. She looked pretty old, and even though she smiled a lot, she seemed tired. Mrs. Eppner had brownish-gray hair, wire-framed glasses, and was very thin. With the brown turtleneck and matching pants she wore, she reminded me of a giant walking stick. She showed me my desk and gave me the books I needed.

"You'll have to excuse me now," Mrs. Eppner said as I put the books in my desk. "I'm going to go grab a cup of coffee." She hadn't asked me anything about myself like I expected a teacher to do. I sat at my desk, which was the first seat in the first row, and stared out into the hall at the kids who were beginning to come in. There is nothing more uncomfortable than having nothing to do and no one to talk with in the middle of a sea of kids.

Everyone who walked into the room looked at me for a few seconds and then walked off. I could hear their whispers behind me, like, "Who's he?" and, "Must be another new student." The knot in my stomach grew larger, tighter, and uglier. Mrs. Eppner might as well have put me on a platform with a sign under me that read, "Please Make the New Kid Feel Weird."

I thought about the things Dad had said that morning and prayed, "Please help me, Jesus." Then things got worse. My neighbor Josh walked in. "Hey," he bellowed, "it's the new kid." He walked up and tousled my hair. "Hat hair!" he announced. Then he loudly whispered, "Better comb it or someone might mistake you for a rooster."

I wanted to run home and never come back. I prayed some more: "Lord Jesus Christ, help me. Pleeease."

Mrs. Eppner returned. The final bell rang. "OK, class,"

she said, "let's settle down. Josh, I've told you before not to eat your lunch until lunchtime. Put it away."

"I was just making sure my mom didn't put catsup on my sandwich again," he said, crumbs spewing out of his mouth as he spoke. From across the room he threw his lunch sack on the shelf above the coat rack. "Two points!" he yelled.

"Josh, it's too early for a visit to the principal's office, don't you think?" Mrs. Eppner said. She smiled weakly at me. "We have a new student today. I'll let him introduce himself after we take attendance, so everyone sit, please." She quickly ran through the names. Everyone called "here" after their names except Josh. He stood up, saluted, and yelled, "Yo!" and plunked back down. Mrs. Eppner ignored it.

Mrs. Eppner turned to me. "This is Aaron Ajax, everyone. Aaron, you are the fourth new student this year. I've never had so many new students come during the year in all my thirty-five years of teaching. Please stand up and tell everyone where you're from and what brings you here."

Knowing there were other fairly new students helped me relax. "I'm from Kalispell, Montana," I began.

"Did he say, 'Can-you-spell Montana?'" Josh yelled from his seat in the middle of the classroom. Mrs. Eppner gave him a stern look.

"I'm from Kalispell, Montana," I repeated.

Josh laughed loudly. "Cowsmell, Montana? What kind of a name is that for a town?"

"That's enough, Josh," Mrs Eppner said. "You may have your old seat back in front of the class. Please trade desks with Matthew...NOW!"

"Hey," a girl from the back of the room yelled. "I have a cousin who lives in Kalispell." I turned to see who had spoken. It was the girl from the playground who had hit me with a snowball. "Do you know a Jesse Milner?" she asked.

"Know him," I said. "He's my best friend." Then we looked at each other again as if for the first time. "Hey," we both spoke at the same time, "I know you."

"You're Shannon, aren't you?" I said.

Sure enough, we'd actually had a water-balloon fight and went swimming a couple summers ago at Jesse's house. That was in the third grade, so I didn't even recognize her until just that moment.

Mrs. Eppner kept saying, "What a small world!" Soon many of the kids asked questions about Montana and the mountains and why we had moved to Bismarck.

When I told everyone my dad was going to work for a radio station some of them listened to, a whole new round of questions began. The morning show would be called *The Paul and Mark Show: PM in the AM.* The kids seemed to think it was pretty cool to get an inside scoop about the radio station.

Mrs. Eppner looked at her watch and gasped. "My goodness! We've gotten carried away," she said. "Thank you, Aaron, for sharing with us. We need to get math done quickly now before we go to the library."

I sat down and let out a deep breath. I wondered if the worst was over and pulled out my math book.

The kids had been friendly. Shannon was no longer my enemy. Josh was still an enemy, but I wondered if that mattered. One thing for sure, he was the class troublemaker. But did he influence the other kids or did they think he was a jerk?

The knot in my stomach shrunk, but it wasn't completely gone. There was still lunchtime. Where would I sit? Would anyone invite me to sit with them? And then there was recess. Would I be included in whatever games the guys played? I felt like I had passed the first test, but it wasn't over yet.

Chapter 8

A Long Day

I was pretty much caught up in all the subjects we covered during the morning. I was even ahead in math. Kids smiled and talked politely to me during library. Shannon invited me to sit at her table with her friend Molly.

"About the snowball I hit you with on Saturday," she said. "I'm really, really sorry. I was in a bad mood because my parents were fighting. I felt so angry, I guess I took it out on you."

"Ah, don't worry about it," I said, relieved to have someone invite me to sit with them. Still, it would have been nice if one of the guys had done that. I couldn't just hang out with girls if I wanted to fit in.

The rest of the morning went fairly well until just before lunch. We took turns reading out loud while Josh aimed spitballs at me. I tried to ignore him and rested my head between my hands to act as a deflector. Mrs. Eppner looked around suspiciously a couple times, but Josh quickly acted like he was concentrating on the story.

The story was about John Chapman, known as Johnny Appleseed. He was a Christian who planted apple trees throughout Ohio and Indiana for pioneer families. People and animals loved him because he loved them and served them in a number of ways. Johnny Appleseed brought news to people across untamed lands and planted apple trees for them to enjoy for generations to come.

I love reading about heroes who became famous by helping people. One of my favorite books at home is a saints' book for boys. Stories about Saint John Bosco, who built schools for boys; Saint Martin de Porres, who served the poor and sick; Saint Maximilian Kolbe, who spread the Gospel through newspapers and gave his own life in exchange for another man to be spared in a concentration camp; and so many others who inspire me. Ordinary people accomplish amazing things when they let God work through them.

Reading about Johnny Appleseed, I really liked that he was just an average guy. He dressed and acted kind of goofy in some ways, and yet he did something great. Planting apple seeds, one by one, seemed like a small thing at the time, but over the course of many years, he became well known and loved. And thanks to him, thousands of people enjoyed fruit from all the trees he planted.

I tried to concentrate on the story, but the spitballs bouncing off the side of my head irritated me. What could I do to get him to stop? I took a notebook out of my desk and held it to the side of my head as a shield.

Mrs. Eppner suddenly interrupted the reading. "Just a minute, class. Aaron, why is that notebook on the side of your head?"

I froze. It would serve Josh right if I told on him, but who wants to be a tattler? "The light is a little bright in my eyes," I said. I wanted to get Josh in trouble, but I didn't dare.

"And is the light dropping little wads of paper on you, Aaron?" Mrs. Eppner asked. This was insane. Why should I get into trouble protecting Josh?

"No," I answered. Mrs. Eppner stood staring into my eyes. I couldn't believe it. She was angry. I had no desire to protect Josh. "Can't *you* figure it out for yourself?" I asked.

Mrs. Eppner's brow immediately wrinkled into a deep frown and her jaw clenched. "No, I can't, smart guy, so I guess *you* will have to tell me." She had taken my question the wrong way. I hadn't meant to sound disrespectful.

What could I do? I had to tell her. "Josh is shooting spit wads at me," I said quietly. The knot in my stomach I began the day with returned as large as a boulder now. I felt weak from anger and embarrassment. Josh glared at me.

"Josh, you may take your seat in the principal's office. Kindly take Mr. Ajax with you. Talking back to a teacher is not the best way to start your first day at school," she said. "As a matter of fact, it's almost lunchtime, so you two boys may take your lunch to the office with you. Tell Mr. Kramer I'll meet him there just before the lunch period is over." I swallowed back tears that threatened to break loose. All I needed now to make things worse was to cry in front of everyone. Shaking, with an aching lump in my throat, a boulder-sized knot in my stomach, and what must have certainly been a fire-red face, I followed Josh out of the room and down the hall.

"Nice going," he said. "You aren't too bright, are you?"

"Oh, shut up!" I said angrily. "You deserve to be going to the principal's office. I don't. So get off my case!" Josh's face dropped. He looked surprised.

Mr. Kramer, the principal, was standing just outside his office when we approached. "Boys, I heard someone say 'shut up.' That is not how to show respect for each other. Are you coming to see me?"

"Yes," we both said.

He put his arms around our shoulders and steered us into his office. "Judging by the looks on your faces, I assume Mrs. Eppner didn't send you here to cheer me up." He spoke sternly but in a friendly sort of way. "Looks like lunch with the principal again, am I right, Josh?" Josh looked at Mr. Kramer and then down at the floor and nodded. "You know, Josh, you've only been here a few weeks and already I've had more lunches with you than I've had with my wife this month. Was your last principal so lucky?"

I couldn't believe it. Josh was one of the new kids! My dad slipped the fact that he got into trouble at school when he was the new kid. Was that why Josh acted like such a jerk? I wondered if my dad was anything like Josh as a kid.

We had to eat our lunch in silence and miss lunch recess. When Mrs. Eppner arrived, I had a chance to explain that I hadn't meant to be disrespectful.

"Maybe I was too short-tempered," she said apologetically. "I just don't need another class troublemaker." She looked over at Josh. "Josh, I've tried to be patient with you. I'm giving you an in-school suspension. You'll spend the rest of the day in the office and all day tomorrow. I'll give you your assignments to do. Your parents will need to call me before you may return to class on Wednesday. Do you understand?"

Josh looked at the floor and nodded. I almost felt sorry for him. That feeling evaporated, however, the moment he looked up and gave me a dirty look. Mrs. Eppner and I returned to class, leaving Josh sitting and staring at the floor.

The afternoon crawled by. I felt slow and tired from the stress of the day. We had gym class in the afternoon, so there was no recess. It only meant putting off the reality of fitting in on the playground, but I was happy for the delay. Recess would be tomorrow's problem.

Kids were friendly enough during gym class, but I could see everyone had their own group of friends. I couldn't figure out the situation since we were kept mostly occupied in a game of kickball, but it was obvious there were two main groups. Mike and Gary were leaders. Gary seemed the nicest. He was athletic and generally decent to the other kids. Mike was athletic too, but he insulted people a lot. Some of the kids followed along, adding their own comments to his.

Shannon and Molly talked with me while we waited in line for our turn to kick the ball. Some of the other girls giggled and acted weird around me, making me uncomfortable. I didn't know if I should actually say something or ignore them. I just talked with Shannon and Molly.

Back in class, we did spelling. I'm as bad at spelling as I'm good at math, and I'm really good at math. I won the state math-o-rama in Montana two years in a row. By the time the 3:00 o'clock bell rang, I had been at school for seven hours, but it felt like twenty. I walked home down the alley. All I wanted to do was get home and lie on the couch. Mrs. Murples, our next-door neighbor, had a little white dog that ran over to the fence and barked. He seemed friendly, so I stopped to pet him.

Then I heard a familiar bark coming from the next yard. Waggles jumped on the fence, trying to get to me. Good old Waggles. I ran over and let him out of the gate. Even though he was not supposed to jump up, I let him jump all over me and lick my face.

When I walked into the house with Waggles, my mom complained he had muddy paws, so I took a towel and wiped them off. Luke was already home, telling everyone about his day. Tyler ran over with Snoopy in one arm and wrapped his other arm around me.

"Air-yun! I missed you," he said. "I didn't even play with your toys while you were gone, and Mom already cleaned up the juice I spilled on your bed." Normally I would have yelled, "What were you doing in my room?" But instead, it just felt good to sit on the couch and hug him.

Mom and Dad wanted to know how my day went. I didn't want to talk about it, but you know how it is with parents. They always want to know about school, so especially on my first day, I had to tell them something.

"Well, let's see," I said. "A girl who threw a snowball at me on Saturday apologized, so that's good. The kid who hates me got sent to the principal's office. That's good. I got sent with him. That's bad. The teacher apologized for sending me. That's good. I'm not friends with any of the boys yet, so that's bad. All in all," I summed up, "it was a good and bad day, and I'm too tired to talk much right now."

I knew my parents would want the details after dinner, but for now, they let it go. Dad announced he was going to get back to painting the front entryway. Mom wanted to know who wanted to go to the store with her to buy groceries. "I do," Tyler and Luke both yelled. They grabbed their coats and headed to the car. Then Mom ran around looking for her car keys.

"I thought I put them in my purse, but they aren't here," she said, looking around on the kitchen counters and in drawers. The kitchen adjoined a dining room on one side and a family room on the other. I sat on the couch, watching Mom search. My hand felt some keys between the two cushions. "Is this what you're looking for?" I asked, jingling them.

"Oh, you're my hero!" Mom cried. She grabbed the keys, hugged me, and was out the door. I slumped down on the couch, her last word—*hero*—echoing in my mind. It was that word that gave me an idea. It seemed like a good one at the time, but then, isn't that the way it usually is with ideas that get you into trouble?

Chapter 9

Saint or Sinner?

It was probably the combination of reading about Johnny Appleseed and my mom's referring to me as a hero that gave me the idea. My love of saints' stories also must have been a part of it.

Not only did I always admire heroes and saints, but I think, like most kids, I wanted to *be* one. I'm guessing that most kids imagine what it would be like to be a hero—the one who saves the day.

When I was little, I loved all the usual superheroes. As I got older, I realized that flying through the air, seeing through walls, or climbing the outside of buildings was not actually possible for people. But when I began reading the Bible and learning about the saints, it hit me that Jesus was the greatest hero of all times. He's not make-believe either, he's God. Walking on water, calming storms, healing the sick, bringing the dead back to life, rising from the dead... nothing is impossible for him.

Then there's the saints. They loved God so much that they lived heroic lives. For instance, Saint Isaac

Jogues, one of my favorites, was a Jesuit priest from France. He came to the New World in the early 1600s to teach the Indians about Jesus. When he was captured by the Mohawks, they did horrible things to him—like cutting off the ends of his fingers off and making him a slave. After years of cruel treatment, Father Jogues escaped and returned to France. I would have kissed the ground and spent the rest of my life in retirement. I might have written a book about my adventures and then lived a nice, quiet life.

That's not what Saint Isaac Jogues did, however. He went back to the people who had deformed and tortured him. He did it out of love for Jesus. Even though the Mohawks had treated him so cruelly, Father Jogues knew that Jesus still loved them and he wanted them to know who Jesus was.

Some of the saints, like Francis of Assisi, became so well known that thousands of people flocked to see them while they were still on earth. After Saint Francis received the stigmata (that's when God gives a person the actual wounds Christ received on the cross), people came from all over just to see him.

You probably wonder where I'm going with all this. I want to give you a little background so you'll understand how my mind was working. First of all, I admired saints. Many of them were misunderstood, suffered, and were hated. I felt I was often misunderstood. I was suffering by having to move and go to a new school, and I was certainly hated by Josh. When my mom called me a hero, it clicked for me that becoming a hero was actually a lifelong dream of mine.

I knew saints were heroes, but were all heroes saints? I wasn't sure about that one. Johnny Appleseed became a famous hero, but was he a saint? He was a nice guy and he loved God, so I thought he probably was. At any rate, I figured the saint part would follow naturally while I became well known for doing good in the world. Energized by my plan, I threw my coat and hat on and yelled to my dad that I was going out for some fresh air.

"Take Waggles for a walk as long as you're going," he said. I wasn't sure how to get started, but I felt the need to get outside to put my plan into action. Looking back, I realize my first move should have been to pray. I was thinking about being a saint, or at least some kind of hero, and I forgot to include God in my plan.

Right away, I noticed an elderly man across the street taking groceries out of his car. I ran over and introduced myself and offered to carry in his groceries for him. He looked so pleased it made me feel good inside. He thanked me at least ten times and insisted on giving me a candy bar. I slipped it into my pocket for later.

Back outside, nothing seemed to be going on. I walked up and down a couple blocks until I noticed a plastic garbage-can lid blowing on my block. *Better than nothing,* I thought. I knocked on the door to the house where I guessed it belonged.

"I'm not buying anything," the lady who answered the door said.

"Oh, I'm not selling anything. I was just wondering if this lid is yours?"

"What are you talking about?" She squinted her eyes at me and started to close the door a little. "Is this some kind of joke?"

"No," I said. "I found this garbage-can lid near your house, so I wondered if it was yours."

"Uh, no," she said. "Finders, keepers, so why don't you just keep it?" Then she closed the door. I guess she was a little confused.

Now I didn't know what I should do with the lid. I didn't want to just leave it on the ground somewhere. *Well,* I thought, *sometimes a hero in a movie has to do some detective work.* I walked down the alley to see if anyone's garbage can was missing a lid.

I noticed Mrs. Murples' little white dog, Frisky, staring at me through the fence from a couple houses away. I laid the lid down and walked over to pet him. Waggles and Frisky sniffed each other and wagged their tails. "Hi, Frisky," I said, putting my hand through the fence to scratch under his neck.

Since things were progressing so slowly, the idea came to me to create situations where I could be the hero. For instance, if Frisky were to escape through the gate, Mrs. Murples would surely be worried about him. And if I found him and returned him to her, she would certainly appreciate my good deed.

My heart raced. What if someone noticed me unlatching the gate? I looked around. I didn't think anyone would see me, but what kind of hero caused the problem he later solved? I reasoned that this was just to get me started. It wouldn't hurt anyone, and maybe it would actually help. Mrs. Murples might decide to put a lock on the gate, which she should probably do anyway. Any kid or dognapper could easily open the gate and take Frisky. A cute dog like Frisky might even be valuable. He looked part poodle. Yes, I decided, I actually was doing a good deed.

I unlatched the gate. Frisky came out willingly. He and Waggles circled each other a few times, and then Frisky started to run down the alley. Now my heart really raced. What if I caused him to actually run away? "Here, Frisky!" I called. "Here, boy!"

Frisky turned to look at me briefly, then continued down the alley. "Frisky, come!" I yelled. Frisky had no intention of coming. He ran to the end of the alley and turned into the neighborhood, keeping at least five houses ahead of me. I let Waggles off his leash, hoping he would catch up to Frisky and get him to stop. Waggles stayed at my side while I ran. When Frisky noticed me running, he ran too, staying safely ahead.

What have I done? I wondered. If Frisky gets lost or hit by a car, it will be my fault. I ran, and Frisky kept ahead of me until we were about seven blocks from home.

A police officer driving by slowed and rolled down his window. "Don't you know the city has a leash ordinance?" he called out. "You can't have those two dogs running around loose like that."

"I know," I said between pants. "The white one is

my neighbor's. He escaped, and I'm trying to catch him."

Once the police officer understood the situation, he drove ahead and pulled into a driveway to block Frisky's path. As soon as he got out of the car and called to him, Frisky went right over to him, wagging his tail. He held him by his collar. "Here you go," he said. "Do you live far from here?"

When I told him about seven blocks, he asked if I'd like a ride back in the police car. "Yes, that would be fantastic!" I answered. My heart pounded partly from all the running and partly from the excitement. *This is amazing,* I thought, looking at the neighborhood from the inside of a police car.

"Your neighbor is lucky to have you looking out for her dog," he said. "Otherwise, he might have been hit by a car or picked up as a stray." A shiver went down my spine at the thought of the trouble I could have caused. Instead, here I was, a hero riding home in a squad car.

Mrs. Murples was outside calling for Frisky when we pulled up. She came running to the car when she saw him in my arms. "Oh, my baby!" she cried. "Where did you find him?"

The police officer explained how he had found me running after Frisky. Mrs. Murples hugged me and took Frisky into her arms. I realized that everything he said was the truth. I never even lied. There was a small part of me that felt guilty. It was my conscience telling me what a jerk I was to almost cause Frisky to get lost and then take credit for saving him. I ignored it. Both the police officer and Mrs. Murples made a big deal about what a great guy I was. My plan had worked—sort of. Mrs. Murples insisted on giving me a plate of cookies and five dollars as a reward.

The small guilty feeling grew larger. I pushed the feeling out of my mind, however, when she told me she was going to put a lock on her gate. I convinced myself that I had actually done a good deed. Without me, Frisky might have one day really gotten lost.

My parents made a big fuss when Waggles and I came home with the cookies, the money, and an explanation as to why I had been riding in a police car. I tossed a cookie to Waggles and whispered, "Even though you don't deserve it. You were no help at all."

"You'll ruin your appetite for supper," Mom warned, "and you know that Waggles gets sick when he eats sweets. Put the plate on the counter for now."

With all the attention and rewards, the guilty feeling shrunk. By the time supper was over, I didn't even notice it. Then I got to thinking that I needed to keep this hero thing going. So once again, I set up a situation and convinced myself that it was actually in everyone's best interest.

Tyler became my helper. I had noticed a skeleton key on the top shelf of the medicine cabinet in the second-floor bathroom. Most of the inside doors were as old as the house—ninety years old. They had key holes for skeleton keys.

I knew from my own childhood that it's not unusual for a small kid to lock himself in a bathroom. I told Tyler to lock himself in and call for help. When everyone panicked, thinking the key was still in the bathroom, I would save the day and pull it out of my pocket. I hadn't decided if I should act like I had a strange feeling I would be needing it or if I should say I had been looking at it and absentmindedly put it in my pocket instead of returning it to the shelf.

The important thing, I told myself, is that Tyler could actually lock himself in. The key *should* be kept somewhere safe outside the bathroom in case of such an event. By setting up this rescue mission, I was helping to avoid a real tragedy, I decided.

After giving Tyler his instructions, I walked downstairs. Dad was making a fire in the fireplace, and Mom and Luke were watching. Perfect. Everyone would be able to hear Tyler when he started yelling.

"Where's Tyler?" Mom asked as I came down the stairs. I wasn't expecting that. I decided that as long as I didn't lie, setting up these scenarios wasn't dishonest at all.

"Oh, he's upstairs doing something," I said.

"Doing what?" Mom persisted. "Maybe you'd better go check on him."

I wished Tyler would hurry up and yell for help. "OK, sure, Mom. Let me just get a drink first. I'm real thirsty." I had just lied. I wasn't thirsty. Oh well, being thirsty or not probably isn't important enough to count as a real lie, I decided. Anyway, I *am* trying to help my family.

"Help me! Help me! I'm dying!" Tyler cried from upstairs.

Finally! I thought, though I never told him to say he was dying. *I hope he doesn't blow it.*

Everyone ran upstairs. "Help me, Air-yun! Snoopy and I need saving," he yelled. "Quick! I can't breathe! I'm drowning!"

"Tyler, open the door and come out," Dad said.

"I'm not supposed to," Tyler answered.

"What are you talking about?" Dad asked. "Open the door."

"Air-yun said not to," Tyler replied. "And I tried, but it doesn't open. Only Air-yun can save me."

"What kind of game is this, Aaron?" Mom asked.

"Oh, look," I said. "I happen to have the key in my pocket." I stuck the key in the door but couldn't click the lock.

"What are you doing?" Mom asked. "Why do you have that key? It doesn't go to this door. That's an old key I've had since Kalispell."

"Air-yun, what's taking so long? You said I would be out in a jiffy." Tyler didn't let up. "Save me before I get eaten by the sharks! Help! Air-yun, come quick!"

Everyone stood and stared at me. "What's going on?" Dad demanded. My mind went blank. I couldn't think of any way to cover up. "Well?" he said.

In the meantime Tyler kept up his screaming. "How are we going to get him out of there?" I asked, realizing there were no hinges to unscrew on the outside of the door. Mom began explaining to Tyler what he needed to do to unlock the door. After several tries, he opened it and ran into Mom's arms.

"Air-yun, your big idea didn't work bery well," Tyler cried. Everyone turned toward me and waited for an explanation.

"This should be interesting," Luke said. I paused, desperately trying to figure out how to talk my way out of this. No bright ideas popped into my head. There was nothing left to do but tell the truth.

I started from the beginning. I included the bad parts of my school day and how the idea of being a saint—or at least some kind of a hero—seemed like a great idea. I explained that I had thought it would be a way to rise above my problems to a better life.

My parents listened patiently. Luke and Tyler had gotten bored halfway through and went to play in their room. Dad spoke first. "Real heroes don't cause problems and then act like they've saved the day," he said. "It's not honest."

"And saints don't have the goal of bringing attention to themselves," Mom said. "Their goal is to do the will of God and give glory to him, not to themselves. The saints were serving God through serving others."

Dad put his arm around me. "Dishonesty is never God's way. Your job in life is to seek to do God's will, whatever that might be. Every morning you should ask God to guide you during the day."

Everything they said made sense. How could I have been so foolish? I had been more interested in helping myself look important than in serving God or helping people.

"I guess I'd better give Mrs. Murples' cookies and money back to her," I said.

"You can't give back the cookies," Mom said. "They're almost gone. You do need to return the money and be honest with her. It's too late to go over there now, it's almost bedtime. Tomorrow after school you can talk to her. You will also help me bake Mrs. Murples a loaf of bread to replace the cookies."

Lying in bed that night, I recalled the events of the day. Returning the five dollars would be embarrassing, but still I felt relieved. I admitted to myself that I never really felt like a true hero and definitely not a saint.

"Dear God," I prayed. "I'm sorry for all my dishonesty. I am sorry I used people to look important. Please help me to put you first in my life. And please, God, even though I haven't been very good today, help me to fit in at school."

Chapter 10

Back to School

We ate breakfast the next morning while listening to the PM *in the* AM radio show. It was my dad's first day at work. He did the news and then interacted with Mark the rest of the time. While Mom left the room to put in a load of laundry, Mark announced a listener contest. Three people would call in and compete by putting their face in a sink of water and singing "Row, Row, Row Your Boat," holding their phones close enough to be heard. The winner would receive dinner for two at a local restaurant.

Luke ran to the sink and began filling it with water. "I do this all the time in the bathtub, so I know I can win," he said. "You hold the phone for me." I kept dialing the number but kept getting a busy signal. Luke was practicing when Mom walked in.

"Luke! What are you doing with your face in a sink full of water? You are supposed to be getting ready for school!"

"It's not what it looks like," I said. "We're competing in a radio contest to win a free dinner for you and Dad."

"Family members of employees cannot enter the contests," she said.

"What?" Luke said. "Then we should be listening to some other radio station."

"Don't be ridiculous, Luke. Now dry up all this water and finish getting ready."

After morning prayers, Luke and I left for school. "Don't you feel stupid wearing a ski mask?" I asked him.

"No," he said. "Don't you feel stupid taking money and cookies from little old ladies?"

"Did you have to remind me? I was trying not to think about it," I said. "It's bad enough that I have to go back to school and try to fit in. Why don't you ever have any problems fitting in?"

Luke stopped and looked at me. "Are you kidding?" he said. "Don't you remember how I used to put my head down and ignore people in kindergarten because I was so shy? Now that I'm older, I just smile a lot and usually people smile back, and then one of us starts talking." He resumed walking. "And besides, I pray whenever I need help with something."

"But don't you ever feel like God sometimes doesn't answer your prayers?" I asked.

"Nope. It hasn't happened yet," he answered.

I was about to tell Luke he needed to wake up and realize you don't always get what you pray for, but we were at school and the final bell rang. We ran to our classrooms. I was late, so Mrs. Eppner sent me to the principal's office for a tardy slip.

"Don't get into the late habit, Aaron," she warned.

Josh sneered at me from his chair when he saw me in the office. Mr. Kramer looked up from his desk when I asked the secretary for a tardy slip. "Well, good morning, Aaron. Now after today, I don't want to see you in my office again unless it's to bring me a present on my birthday."

I walked back to class and handed my slip to Mrs. Eppner. Math had already begun, so I took my seat. Mrs. Eppner asked me to go to the board to do one of the problems. When I got that one right, she had me do another and then another. She kept making them harder, trying to trip me up.

"Well, we have a little math genius, I see."

As I returned to my seat I heard Mike say under his breath, "Here comes Mr. Math." A couple kids around him snickered. The old knot in my stomach was alive and well.

I thought I was at least safe from the playground until lunchtime, but I was wrong. We had missed a midmorning recess the day before because of library. Everyone hurried to the coat rack to get their things. Mike grabbed a football from the shelf and tossed it to another boy.

"Wait until you are outside," Mrs. Eppner said. She sounded tired. "And make sure you line up to come back in as soon as you hear the bell."

All the kids ran onto the playground. I was the last

one out the door. I looked for Shannon and Molly, figuring it was better to talk with a couple girls than stand around by myself. They were nowhere to be seen. The boys were all playing football.

I walked over to where the game was being played. No one asked me to join. My biggest fear had arrived. I was alone in a sea of kids.

I walked around on the outskirts of the game and instinctively shot up a quick prayer, asking God to help me with this awkward situation. Then I stood on the sidelines, watching. Gary looked over at me. "Are you any good?" he asked.

"I'm OK, I guess," I answered. My stomach was heavy with the big knot filling it. I was so nervous I wondered if I could even catch the ball. Gary told me to join his team since they were one guy short anyway. He tossed me the ball.

"You can hike it," he said, "but I suggest taking your gloves off."

Not until then did I notice no one else was wearing gloves. I pulled mine off and shoved them into my pockets. My hands stung from the cold, but it was a relief to be in the game. I caught one pass and also dropped one later on. Mike had yelled, "Good thing he's on your team and not ours with those slippery hands."

Gary shot back, "Yeah, it's a good thing. You already have enough fumblers." There were a lot of back-and-forth insults but nothing serious. Gary also complimented guys when they made good plays. It

was obvious everyone looked up to him, and not just because he was a head taller than most of us. He had red hair and freckles and smiled a lot. Mike had dark hair and eyes and was average height. He was a leader too, but he used a lot of sarcasm, though again, nothing serious.

When the bell rang, I couldn't believe recess was already over. The knot in my stomach was gone. It had evaporated with all the physical activity and the relief of being included. I tried to get in line near Gary, but he was surrounded by others. Two other guys who had been on my team came up and stood by me. They introduced themselves as Dylan and Matthew. Dylan had moved from Iowa last summer, where his parents used to farm. He looked like I thought a farm boy would look, with brown hair in a choppy cut and thick freckles across his nose. Matthew had been born in Minot, North Dakota, but he had moved around quite a bit before his father retired from the military last year. He had black hair, blue eyes, and a mouth full of braces.

Dylan lived across the street from the school and invited me to come over to his house that afternoon. I immediately said I'd love to, but then I remembered I needed to get home to make bread with my mom and pay Mrs. Murples a visit. "How about tomorrow instead?"

"Tomorrow's Wednesday," Dylan said. "We always have our after-school football game then. It's our team, the Rads, against the Vikings. Are you going to join us?"

"Who are the Vikings?" I asked.

"We just played them," Dylan answered.

"Sure," I said, "I'll be there." Walking back into class, a light, happy feeling replaced the old knot. I was fitting in. The worst must be over. "Thank you, Jesus," I prayed as I sat at my desk, digging out my reading book.

"Today, class," Mrs. Eppner began, "we're going to read about Martin Luther King—a modern-day hero who gave his life for the cause of equality for all people."

Great, I thought, *back to the hero business.* But as we read about this man who fought to end discrimination, I saw things with new eyes. I understood in a deeper way now that a real hero is someone who takes leadership to improve a situation and not someone looking to impress others.

During lunch recess, we played more football. The afternoon flew by. We spent extra time on history (my other favorite subject) in order to put up a time line. Everyone had a chance to add pictures that portrayed various historical events. Walking home from school, it struck me that even though it was only my second day, it had been a pretty good day. I was starting to like Bismarck. I loved our new house, school was turning out OK, and I had two new friends—Dylan and Matthew. Even though I still had to face Mrs. Murples about my dishonesty, I felt OK.

Then I thought of Jesse. If I was in Kalispell, maybe I'd be stopping off at his house after school like I often did. I wondered how Sid Peters was getting around on his crutches. Even though it had been an OK day, thinking of Kalispell felt like a piece of me was still there. I decided to give Jesse another call, but first I needed to go back and clear everything up with Mrs. Murples.

Chapter 11

Mrs. Murples

Mom was waiting for me when I got home. She had all the ingredients for making bread ready on the counter.

"Let's get started right away so it will be done by dinnertime," she said. I had actually never made bread by myself before, although I had helped.

"This stuff might not even be edible by the time I get done with it," I said. Mom informed me that she would supervise. Luke and Tyler decided watching me would be entertaining.

"Can I help when everything gets sticky and you have to play with it?" Tyler asked.

Luke thought he was hilarious by yelling things like, "Oh, no, it said half a cup, not a whole cup! Just kidding," and, "Didn't you see that big egg shell that fell in? Just kidding."

When I complained about my audience, Mom said they weren't hurting me and could watch and learn. I think Tyler was getting a better lesson in how to bother a big brother. Mom did finally tell Luke to keep quiet after he let out a gasp and yelled, "Oh, no! I just remembered, I used this bowl to feed Waggles this morning! Just kidding."

When it came time for kneading the dough, I asked Mom if she had some rubber gloves to avoid getting my hands sticky. She laughed and said rubber gloves were for cleaning, not bread making. The problem is that you can mix the dough with a wooden spoon only so long. It gets heavy and hard to turn, so you need to knead it all around with your hands until it's the right consistency. The way to do this is to keep adding flour and mushing it all around until it's soft and doughy but not sticky.

Getting from the point of sticky to doughy is the gross part. It cakes on your hands like thick slime. Once you become slime-covered, you can no longer touch anything without leaving a mess. Luke offered to sprinkle more flour on while I mixed the dough with my hands. Naturally he had to yell things like, "Look out below," and "Avalanche! Run for cover!" as he poured the flour.

There ended up being enough for four loaves. The loaves had to sit out an hour so they could rise before going into the oven. Mom had used a speedy recipe that only needed to rise once instead of twice. It seems like an awful lot of time and work for something you could just buy at the store.

I did homework until the bread was in the oven. Then I began getting nervous, wondering what I would say to Mrs. Murples. I practiced in my mind:

*Mrs. Murples, I'm the one who let Frisky out of the gate. He looked kinda bored in there...*oops...no, that would be another lie. I wondered how I was going to do this without looking foolish.

When the bread had baked and cooled a little, Mom put it in an air-tight bag and suggested we all say a little prayer to help me. "Dear God," she prayed, "please give Aaron the words he needs. Keep him close to you, and help him to always do what's right."

A cold north wind swirled around the houses and piled snow into drifts. Two inches had fallen that morning, so a lot of people had already shoveled their walks. My fingers were warmed by the bread through the soft plastic as I climbed Mrs. Murples' porch steps. I knocked on her door and waited. Frisky barked from inside. Mrs. Murples' sidewalk and driveway were still covered with snow and there were no footprints, so I knew she was home.

My mind was still blank. *What would I say?* I knocked again. No answer; just Frisky barking. With the biting wind blowing around her porch, I worried the bread and my fingers would both freeze if she didn't answer soon.

I went around to the back door. *Maybe she was in the back of the house and couldn't hear me,* I thought, then realized that Frisky's barking could surely be heard throughout the house. I just wanted to hurry and get it over with. I knocked hard on the back door. Frisky's bark from inside was a lot closer now. *Where is she?* I wondered.

I knocked again and then listened to Frisky's bark. There was a small slit in the curtain. It seemed rude to peek through the slit. I strained my ears to listen in between Frisky's barks.

It seemed like Mrs. Murples was telling me to come in, but I wasn't sure. What if she was just trying to quiet Frisky down because she didn't want visitors today and then I walked into her house? That would be embarrassing. I went ahead and peered through the curtain slit. The back door led to a small entryway for hanging coats and then into the kitchen. I could see a kitchen stove and yellow-painted cupboards, but not much else.

I looked down and saw Frisky barking next to something on the floor. He looked toward the door, barked a couple times, then turned back to the thing on the floor and barked again. The window started to fog up from my breath. I wiped it with my coat sleeve and peered in again. *Why doesn't she just answer the door?* I wondered.

Suddenly a horrible realization hit me. That was Mrs. Murples lying on the kitchen floor! I grabbed the handle on the door, but my hands only slid as I tried to turn it. It was locked.

With my heart beating hard, I ran around to the front door. The handle turned and I shoved my body up against the door to open it. I stepped into the living room and hurried through the doorway that led through the dining room and then into the kitchen. Frisky jumped up on me, barking frantically.

Mrs. Murples was on her back with her eyes closed. "Mrs. Murples!" I yelled, shaking her lightly. Fear shot through me *Was she dead?*

I called her name again and took hold of her hands. They were cold, but it seemed like her fingers moved a little in mine. "Mrs. Murples, can you hear me?"

I looked around and saw a phone on the wall just above her. I stood and leaned over Mrs. Murples' body and reached for it to call 911.

"We need help!" I yelled. "I found my neighbor lying on the floor and I don't know if she's still alive." I didn't even know Mrs. Murples' address, so I gave mine and explained that the house was right next to it to the north.

"We are sending someone right away," the dispatcher said. "Can you tell if she's still breathing?" I looked down and saw Mrs. Murples' eyes flutter open.

"She's opening her eyes!" I yelled. "I'm going to lay the phone down to keep the line open, but I need to go to Mrs. Murples." I laid the phone on the counter and sat down next to Mrs. Murples. She blinked a few times, looking confused.

"It's me, Aaron, your neighbor," I said, laying my hand on her arm. "When you didn't answer your door, I looked through the window and saw you lying here."

Mrs. Murples looked around and then seemed to understand. In a faint voice she whispered, "Oh, Aaron, thank God you're here," she cried. "I slipped on the floor this morning and couldn't get up. I've been praying and praying that God would send someone. You saved Frisky yesterday and now you're saving me."

"Mrs. Murples, I'm not so wonderful. That's why I came over." The words tumbled out. "I felt like an outsider and thought things would be better if I became some kind of a saint or hero. I started out really trying to help people, but then I ended up doing things just to make myself look good." I took a deep breath. "I'm the one who let Frisky out of his yard. He almost ran away before I could catch him and bring him back. I was a big phony. I brought back the five dollars you gave me. My family and I already ate the cookies, but my mom helped me bake a loaf of bread for you."

Tears poured out of her eyes and streamed down the side of her face. "Are you in a lot of pain?" I asked.

Her wrinkled hands wiped at her wet face. "Yes," she admitted, "but that's not why I'm crying. My tears are tears of joy. I was so afraid of never getting found until it was too late."

"Mrs. Murples, if I had not been dishonest yesterday, I wouldn't be here today."

She smiled. "God can use all things for good, so don't you worry, God has big plans for you," Mrs. Murples said. He used you to save my life."

"I didn't do anything special," I said. "I just came here to give you the money and bread."

"You're right," Mrs. Murples agreed. "You didn't do anything special. God did. He answered my prayers, but he used you to do it." She laughed and then cried again. "I guess God isn't ready for me yet."

Mrs. Murples looked into my eyes and squeezed my hand. "Will you pray with me now?" she asked. "I've been asking God for help all day. Now I need to thank him."

I listened to Mrs. Murples give God praise and thanksgiving. Soon an ambulance siren could be heard coming closer. I picked up the phone again. "I guess they're here," I told the dispatcher who was still on the line. "Yes, they're definitely here. They're coming through the door now."

"You did a wonderful job," the dispatcher said, though I insisted I hadn't really done anything. "I'm not just talking about calling us, I'm talking about sitting and comforting her," she said. "Just to let you know, I prayed along from my end."

Wow, I thought, *people are praying all over the place.* Mrs. Murples was lifted onto a stretcher. "Aaron," she called to me, "can you take care of Frisky for me until I can contact my daughter to come and get him?"

"I'd be happy to."

"I can't thank you enough, Aaron," she said. Then she winked at me as she was wheeled toward the door. "And don't you worry about the saint stuff. A lot of them started off on the wrong track. It's where you end up that's important."

As the ambulance drove off, Frisky whimpered. "Don't worry, Frisky," I said. "I'll take care of you. Everything's going to be all right now."

Chapter 12

Real Hero

Everyone's mouth dropped open when I walked in with Frisky in my arms. "I don't believe it," Luke said. "First you took her money, now you took her dog!"

No one had realized the ambulance had stopped at Mrs. Murples' house since they were all in the family room at the back of the house. I explained everything. Waggles and Frisky sniffed each other, and Mom gave them each a chew stick to calm them down. "Let's eat dinner," she said. "I've kept it warm. I wondered what was taking so long, but I figured you and Mrs. Murples must be having a nice talk." Dad said he would call the hospital after dinner to see how Mrs. Murples was doing and ask what else we could do for her.

During dinner the phone rang. It was a reporter from the *Bismarck Tribune*. Mrs. Murples had told everyone at the hospital that she might have died if it wasn't for me. It turned out she had broken her hip, but it looked like a small hairline fracture. The reporter wanted to interview me and take a picture.

I couldn't believe it. I had gotten the idea of being a hero out of my head and now I was going to be written up in the newspaper. Ironically, I hadn't done much of anything. I just happened to be in the right place at the right time.

"Oh, no!" I said as I began clearing the table. "How am I going to explain what I was doing at Mrs. Murples' house?"

"Don't worry, Aaron, I'll help you out," Luke said. "I'll swear to them that you've never stolen dogs or taken money from nice old ladies before in your life. It was just that one time. I'll tell them you even shared the cookies you tricked Mrs. Murples out of."

"Mom! What am I going to do?" I asked.

"Calm down, Aaron," Mom said. "Luke, you will kindly stay out of the interview. Aaron, all you have to say is that you were bringing a loaf of bread over to Mrs. Murples. It's not necessary to tell everything."

"But isn't that a sin of omission—to purposely mislead someone by leaving out part of the truth?"

"You aren't misleading anyone," Dad said. "Taking Mrs. Murples' dog is not part of the story. That's between you, Mrs. Murples, and God, not the newspaper." That was a big relief. I did not want to look like a fool in the paper.

"Oh, the bread," I suddenly remembered. "I left it sitting on Mrs. Murples' porch. I'll run over and get it." I returned as the reporter arrived at our door. She had just talked with Mrs. Murples at the hospital and wondered if I could go back with her so Mrs. Murples and I could get our picture taken together. I brought the bread along.

The next morning, on the front page of the newspaper was a picture of me standing next to Mrs. Murples in her hospital bed. We each had a hand on the bread, which by that time was looking pretty smashed. Dad read the story out loud as we all ate breakfast.

"Aaron Ajax, twelve, was just being neighborly when he brought a loaf of bread over to his next-door neighbor, Edna Murples, late yesterday afternoon," he read.

"Noticing there were no tracks in the snow that had fallen earlier in the day, Ajax became alarmed when no one answered his knocks at the door. That's when this mixture of junior sleuth and angel of mercy decided to force his way inside."

"Dad, what's a junior sleuth? I never called myself an angel of mercy," I said. "And I definitely never said I forced my way in. The door opened right up. Dad, she got it wrong."

"Aaron, a sleuth is like a detective, someone who figures something out. The reporter used her own words to write the story," Dad said. "When one person tells a story to another person, what was in your head and what ends up on paper are not always identical. Now just let me finish.

"Murples had slipped in her kitchen while she was cleaning up from breakfast around 8:00 AM that day. Her hip was fractured in the fall, making it impossible for her to get back up. In pain and fearing no one would find her for days, Murples spent the day in prayer with her faithful dog, Frisky, always at her side.

"At around 5:30 PM, Murples heard a knock at her door. Although she said she yelled for help, the repeated knocking indicated she was not being heard. 'I could hear someone going back down the steps, so I prayed harder than I've ever prayed in my life,' Murples said. 'Then I must have lost consciousness.'

"Ajax had gone to the back and knocked again. He said he thought he heard his neighbor's voice in between dog barks but wasn't sure. That's when he looked in the window and saw Murples lying flat on her back. Realizing she was in trouble, he tried to get in, but the door was locked. He ran around to the front, pushed the door open, and found Murples lying on her back and unresponsive. Ajax immediately called 911.

"Emergency 911 operator Lisa Hoffman said she was impressed with Ajax's ability to stay calm and provide important information. 'I was very impressed with him,' she said. 'After he told me everything I needed to know, he very firmly told me he would keep the line open but that Mrs. Murples needed him more than I did.'

"Rescue personnel reached her home twelve minutes after the call and rushed her to St. Alexius Medical Center, where she is listed in stable condition. According to Dr. Maggie Mathewson, Murples fractured her

hip, was dehydrated, and showing early signs of shock. 'She might not have made it through the night if she had not been found,' Dr. Mathewson stated.

"Like a true hero, Ajax, who is a sixth grader at Will-Moore Elementary, insisted he didn't do anything out of the ordinary. 'I just did what anyone would have done,' he said."

Dad put down the paper. "Here you were, sorry for being a phony hero, and God put you in a position to be a real one. Just remember," Dad added, "let God lead the way." He looked at his watch. "You boys better get going or you'll be late for school."

So much had happened since Monday morning. I couldn't wait to call Jesse that evening and tell him everything that had taken place since I had talked with him just four days ago. Then I remembered, there was still something to worry about—Josh. He would be out of in-school suspension now.

Walking into the classroom that morning, I felt like I belonged. Dylan and Matthew came over to me right away. They had seen the story and picture in the paper and thought it was great. Dylan asked if I would be in the after-school football game. In spite of all the excitement, I had remembered to get permission from my mom to stay for the game.

As the warning bell rang, kids settled into their seats. Josh came running through the door out of breath, tossed his coat and hat on a hook, and had just enough time to walk by my desk and give me a dirty look before sitting down. I told myself that Dylan and Matthew had befriended me, so I wasn't alone now. I had also been included in the recess football games. So how miserable could Josh make my life? I wasn't sure.

Attendance was taken and I concentrated on school. I didn't even think about Josh until Mrs. Eppner announced it was time for recess. I went to the coat rack for my coat and then looked for Dylan or Matthew to stand near in line. Josh pushed past me to get in line. Mrs. Eppner expected students to line up in an orderly fashion at the door before she excused us for recess. I didn't want to risk getting into trouble, so I stood at the back near Molly and Shannon.

"Aaron, do you want to walk around with us on the playground?" Shannon asked. I thanked her, but I was glad to tell her I'd be playing football instead. The boys ran out and split into the same teams as the day before. It turned out that Josh was also on Gary's team. When he noticed me, a scowl clouded his face.

"What's 911 boy doing on the team?" he demanded. "The losers belong on Mike's team."

A voice from the other side shouted out, "Look who's talking, the biggest loser of them all." Josh ignored it, but his face flushed red.

The ball went back and forth for a while with no one scoring. I was close to the end zone and no one was guarding me when Matthew threw me a pass. I caught it easily and turned to run but ended up tripping and dropping the ball.

"I told you he shouldn't be on our team," Josh yelled. "He's as clumsy as a moose. He just tripped over his own feet."

I hadn't tripped over my own feet. Someone had stuck their foot out, and I was pretty sure it was Josh. I wondered why no one seemed to notice it. I looked over at Josh, who had a nasty grin on his face. If I accused my own teammate of tripping me, I might end up making myself look bad. I kept quiet, even after a few people yelled out comments like, "Boy, we could've had it," and, "No one even tackled him."

When recess was over, I walked back toward school with Dylan and Matthew. "Didn't you guys see Josh trip me when I fell with the ball?" I asked. Dylan shrugged his shoulders. Matthew smiled. "So that explains it," he said. "You looked so strange, like you were all of a sudden trying to skip."

I was furious. "What's with this kid Josh, anyway?"

"Well, he sure doesn't like you, that's pretty obvious," Dylan said. "I think he just needs someone to pick on. He's always mouthing off and trying to be funny, but no one thinks he is. No one really likes him. Gary lets him play on our side because he's always nice to the misfits."

At the word *misfits,* we all stopped and looked at one another. "You don't think we're misfits, do you?" Dylan asked.

Matthew thought for a minute. "Nah, I don't think so, unless being new at school makes us misfits, which I suppose it probably does a little."

"Just ignore Josh," Matthew advised. "Everyone else does."

Suddenly, instead of feeling like I wanted to punch him, I felt sorry for him. My dad had slipped that he was once a class clown who got into trouble. Josh had blushed when someone called him a loser. Everyone had feelings. I noticed he walked into school alone. He had no friends.

I didn't exactly feel like being nice to Josh, but

I lost any desire to put him down. He was already down. My own fear of not belonging was still fresh. In only three days I was fitting in. Josh had been here a month and didn't seem to have any friends. Being a loud-mouthed, smart aleck worked against him, but he didn't stop. He was in a trap he had set for himself.

Mrs. Eppner looked angry when we returned from the playground. Her pencil-thin lips looked even thinner than usual because she held them so tightly closed as if she was afraid of what might come out. We quietly took our seats. In her hands was a pile of papers that she purposely dropped on the floor.

"Class," she said, "even though I reviewed Chapter 8 in history with you during school time, these test papers are a disgrace. They belong in the garbage. Shannon," she said, "pick these up and pass them out, please. There were no *A*'s, only one *B*, a few *C*'s, and the rest are *D*'s and *F*'s. And you, Josh," she said in almost a whisper, "you didn't get one right. Now everyone may silently read Chapter 8 over again and you will be retested tomorrow." Mrs. Eppner took a deep breath, then in a tired voice said, "I will not tolerate such a lack of effort from my class. Now, everyone, read."

Shannon handed me my test. It had a big red *C* on the top. Then I happened to look back at Josh. He held his head in his hands over his desk. I couldn't see his face, but his ears were bright red. I felt bad for him from the bottom of my heart. Mrs. Eppner had humiliated Josh in front of everyone.

Mrs. Eppner must have felt bad about what she did. She walked over, put her arm on his shoulder, and whispered something to him. I don't know what she said, but she didn't look angry anymore, just tired. I turned to my book and began reading Chapter 8. It covered the period just before the American Revolution began. It was actually interesting, especially the part about the Boston Tea Party. I wondered why we had done so poorly on the test.

It was easy to get through the chapter in the quiet aftermath of Mrs. Eppner's scolding. Josh kept to himself from then on. He didn't bother making any nasty comments to me or anyone else as far as I could tell. The rest of the day seemed to just drag though. Mrs. Eppner's unhappy attitude had rubbed off on everyone, making us feel about as unhappy about being in school as she seemed to feel.

When the final bell rang, most of the boys grabbed their jackets and backpacks and headed out to the playground for the after-school football game. It was cold enough outside that everyone pulled hats on. A frigid wind stung my face and my fingertips felt numb without my gloves. Gary suggested we all agree to wear gloves since it was so cold. It would be clumsy, but everyone agreed.

The teams were even, though not all the guys had stayed after to play. Mike argued that our team had one extra player, so it wasn't fair. Gary offered to give him Josh. Mike laughed and said never mind, you can have your extra player. I looked at Josh. He just looked into the distance and acted like he didn't know that he had just been insulted.

It was a slow, cold game. Twenty minutes into it, neither side had scored. "At this rate we'll be here until dark," someone complained. Finally, after half an hour of play, everyone agreed that whichever side scored first would be the winners. Right after that agreement, I intercepted a pass Mike threw. I didn't even feel the cold and ran with all my might. I dodged a couple guys and was headed for our goal, which was actually the monkey bars.

I've got it! I thought excitedly when I was just a few feet away. Then the unthinkable happened. I stepped away from a guy who ran toward me, knocked into Josh, fell over him, and dropped the ball. I lay still on the ground, disappointed and angry—very, very angry. He tripped me again! How could he be such an idiot?

I picked myself up and looked next to me, where Josh still lay face-down. My teammates went wild. "What's wrong with you?" someone yelled at Josh. "What a klutz," yelled another and, "What a loser!" My anger subsided when Josh picked his skinned face up off the ground.

"I was trying to guard him," Josh said quietly. "I'm sorry. I didn't mean for that to happen."

"You're off our team," Gary yelled. "You are always messing things up."

Josh looked up at Gary, shocked, but said nothing. In a daze, he stood up and walked away.

"Come on, everybody," Gary said. "We can do it

again." Then he slapped my back and said, "That was almost a great play."

His compliment felt hollow. By the look on Josh's face, I knew he really hadn't meant to trip me. The cold had put everyone on edge. We were all in a hurry to get the game over. I didn't care about the game anymore. Josh's sad face haunted me.

"Hey, Josh, wait up," I called.

"You can't quit, Ajax," Gary said.

"He didn't mean it," I said over my shoulders. "Don't you guys ever make mistakes?"

"If you quit, you're off the team too," Gary yelled.

I turned around and looked at everyone. Gary's eyes glared into mine, his chin pushed forward. Jacob and Matthew just stood wide-eyed. Some of the others mumbled things like, "Let him go," and, "Just forget him if he wants to quit."

I ran to catch up with Josh and didn't turn back again. "Josh, I'll walk with you," I said, breathless as much from running as from the shock at what I had just done—separated from the others to be with a guy who had been heartless to me.

Josh stopped and turned around. He looked like a scared rabbit. "What do you want?" he asked, his voice cracking.

"I know you didn't mean to trip me. It's too cold to play football," I answered. "I thought we could walk home together. After all, we live right next-door."

Josh's face softened. "Why would you want to walk with me? I've been a jerk to you since we met."

"Yeah, no kidding," I said. "But we Catholics, well we *are* Christians, you know."

We walked together in silence until we got to the end of our alley. "Want to come in for a while and do something?" I invited him.

A slow smile spread across Josh's face. "Sure," he said, probably sounding more excited than he meant to. "Just let me tell my mom where I'll be." He turned in the direction of his house, then stopped and turned back. "I'm sorry I was such a jerk to you," he said. "I don't know why I did it."

"Forget it," I said. "We can start over."

Josh came over and we discovered we both loved chess. We played for about an hour until it was time for dinner. I enjoyed his company. No kidding. Once he let down his tough-guy exterior, he was actually a lot of fun.

I asked Josh why he put so much energy into getting people mad at him. "I don't know," he said. "This is our third move in two years, and every move gets worse. My dad seems to think he won't get transferred with his company again, but things have gone so awful here, I was hoping he *would* just so I could start over somewhere else."

"I was praying we wouldn't have to leave Montana, but we ended up coming to Bismarck anyway," I laughed.

Josh was quiet a moment and then said, "Maybe God wants me to learn to work my way out of the trouble I've gotten myself into." He thought another minute and added, "And maybe he wanted me to learn what being a Christian is all about." Josh smiled slyly.

We laughed. His sincerity embarrassed me a little. My mom came in and announced it was time for dinner, so Josh needed to leave. He went to the door, turned, and said, "Thanks again, Aaron. You're my first friend in Bismarck."

At dinner, I told everyone about what a pain Josh had been and about the football game. I also admitted that now I was once again dreading going to school. I had walked away from new friends to be with the guy who had treated me horribly. Was I nuts or what? Still, I felt good about my choice.

"You know," Dad said, "think about what has happened in the last couple days. First, you set out to be a hero but by using deceit and seeking to serve yourself. Then, because God placed you in the right place at the right time, Mrs. Murples and the newspaper made you out to be a hero. But now, by walking away from your social position to help a boy in need, you are a real hero regardless of how the others may look at you."

After dinner, I called Jesse. My last call to him had felt like a life-line to my far-away best friend. The call had helped lift me up from feeling like such a loser. This time, it was different. I was excited to tell him how much had happened since we last spoke.

"You've got to be kidding," Jesse said when I filled him in on everything. "Your life sounds so exciting compared to mine. We all signed Sid's cast this week and had a lot of snow yesterday, but other than that, I can't think of anything new around here."

It was good to hear Jesse's voice again, but when I got off the phone, there was not an ache in my heart like there had been the last time. Then I thought of returning to school the next day. I swallowed hard and thought, *Well, I guess I'll just have more to tell Jesse by tomorrow.*

Chapter 13

Home Sweet Home

Walking into school on Thursday felt like playing the Candy Land game as a little kid when I was just about to get to the gingerbread house but instead drew the plum card and had to go back to the beginning. Or the Chutes and Ladder game when that long chute just before the finish dropped me back near start.

I thought I had gotten through the worst of being the new kid at school, but now I had slipped back to start. Possibly, it was even worse than starting over. I was just starting to fit in when I had the nerve to walk out on a football game and get everyone mad at me. The good feeling for doing the right thing was replaced with a "what now?" feeling.

I walked into the classroom earlier than I wanted to be. Luke was in a hurry to get to school that morning because he had been selected as "Thursday Boy." I guess it's like being student of the week but the name of the day is used because that's what the students all voted for. (Remember, this is third grade we're talking about.) He would get to do exciting things like turn on the classroom lights and take the attendance sheet to the office.

As a result of having to walk to school with Thursday Boy, I was one of the first kids to arrive in class. That meant I would be at my desk, forced to face every angry guy who came into the classroom. I would rather have been one of the last to arrive so class could get under way without me having to face anyone.

Dylan came in first. Sticking my head in a history book, I pretended to do some last-minute studying for the test. "Hey, you don't need to do that," Dylan said. "I saw Mrs. Sommers in the hall. She's one of the substitutes, and she told me Mrs. Eppner won't be in today."

"Oh, is that right?"

Dylan then left to hang up his coat. No mention about the football game. He came back just as Matthew walked in. They walked over to me together.

"About yesterday," Matthew began slowly. He and Dylan looked at each other for a moment. Then Matthew said, "Why don't you tell him."

"Well," Dylan said, "after you left, the game ended. No one felt like playing anymore."

"Do you think everyone will still be mad at me today?" I asked.

Dylan answered, "I think most of us were just cold and on edge and—"

Matthew interrupted. "I think we were mostly mad at ourselves. Josh may be a pain, but I don't think anyone really wanted to hurt the guy. You did the right thing."

"Yeah," said Dylan, "even after the way he treated you, you did the right thing."

"Anyway," said Matthew, "I don't know how everyone else feels, but we decided that if you get kicked off the team, we're off too. We're going to stick by you."

I blinked my eyes very quickly. I had heard of people crying for joy, but this was the first time I experienced my eyes watering up over happiness. "Thanks," was all I could think to say.

Gary walked in. He walked right over to me. Knowing that Dylan and Matthew were on my side, I was no longer afraid. If he kicked me off his team for quitting, at least I wouldn't be alone.

He smiled and slapped my back. "Hey, Aaron, sorry about yesterday."

"What?" I asked. I wasn't expecting that.

"About yesterday...maybe it was the cold, I don't know, but I'm not proud of the way I acted. Anyway, if that's how you treat your enemies, I'd be proud to be one of your friends."

All this sentimental talk was embarrassing. It was a good kind of embarrassment—not like discovering you had walked around all day with spaghetti sauce on your face. But it did feel awkward to be made a big deal out of. So it was actually a relief when Mike walked in and joked about it.

"Hey, there's the smart guy," he said. "Ajax was the

only one bright enough to get out of the cold. If it wasn't for him, we might still be out there."

"Yeah, he's obviously smarter than the rest of us," Gary said.

Mike laughed. "Of course we could have kept going, but I knew your team must have been suffering." Then he changed the subject. "Hey, did you guys hear we have a substitute? I wonder if that means no history test."

"I doubt that," Gary said. "Mrs. Eppner probably told the sub to give it to us. She was pretty mad yesterday."

Just then, Josh walked in. "Hey, Josh," Mike called. "Did you hear we have a sub today? I think maybe Mrs. Eppner is sick of us."

"No kidding," he said. "Well, I studied for the test, so I'm ready for anything."

And just like that, Josh began to fit in. No kidding. The day before had been a turning point. A lot of emotions had come out at the football game, and people had had time to think about it. Everyone was making an effort to be nice to one another now, especially to me and Josh.

It was only my fourth day at Will-Moore, and yet it seemed more like a year had gone by. So since it's taken me an entire book to explain one week, I'm going to summarize the rest of the story.

Josh did become just one of the guys. He still had a smart mouth sometimes, but he stopped coming up with all the nasty comments. By the end of the school year, I think everyone mostly forgot about his bad start. Dylan, Matthew, Josh, and I became best friends. We all played chess every Wednesday night at the tournaments held in the library basement.

In case you're wondering, we did have our Chapter 8 history test that Thursday. I got an *A*-. I would have gotten a full *A* if I had remembered that the name of the guy who helped Paul Revere warn the colonists that the British were coming was William Dawes.

Mrs. Eppner never came back to school to teach. She decided to retire early, but she did come back to say goodbye about a week after she left. She explained to everyone that since she was a little girl, she had always wanted to be a teacher. For thirty-five years she had loved it. But now, during year thirty-six, she had some health problems and was finding herself impatient at times. Mrs. Eppner told us the time had come for her to retire. She was going to move to Arizona to be with her daughter and two grandchildren. She opened a bookstore and named it after one of her favorite historical figures—Johnny Appleseed's. Yeah, funny isn't it?

We got a new teacher—Mrs. Petersen. She really knows how to make learning fun. When we studied amphibians during science class, we walked into the room one day and found a tank full of live frogs, salamanders, and toads. For history class, we reenacted parts of the American Revolution. We had a Boston Tea Party and a Boston Massacre. I played the part of William Dawes when it came time for Paul Revere

6th Grade

(played by Josh) to warn the colonists of Massachusetts that the British were coming. I don't think I'll ever forget his name again.

Things have gone well at home also. My dad's radio program, *PM in the AM,* has become a top-rated show. Mom still writes articles, but now she's working on a book too. Luke ran away to join the circus. Just kidding. Luke is his usual happy-go-lucky self. Right now he is praying for a St. Bernard. He's been begging my parents for one and hanging pictures of St. Bernards all over the house. I told him not to expect God to give him everything he asks for since it might not be what's best for him. Luke is not listening, though. Maybe he'll go through something like I did soon when there's no St. Bernard. Or who knows, seeing the way things usually turn out for Luke, maybe we'll find a St. Bernard on our doorstep some morning.

Tyler continues to be my cute little buddy. He stopped calling me Air-yun about a month ago and learned to actually say Aaron. I'm very proud of him now that he's almost five and seems to be getting accomplished at the art of pestering his older brother. The good news in this case is that I'm not the target.

The best family news of all is that my mom is expecting another baby in a few months. Tyler is still trying to convince my parents to name him or her Snoopy.

The next time I called Jesse, all the sadness over our separation was gone. Instead, I was excited to tell him how school was going and about the new baby.

I can see that time and distance have changed our friendship in some ways, but we'll always be each other's first best friend.

Speaking of changes, it's a good time to sum up the spiritual aspect of this story, which is really the reason I wanted to write it all down. Granted, moving to a new home is not the end of the world, but it's a big deal in a kid's life. The hardest part was losing my faith in prayer, wondering what the point of praying was if God didn't answer it. I now understand that we can do the asking, but God does the directing. Prayer is about us uniting ourselves with God's will and not the other way around. We just need to keep asking for his help along the way and accept his plan for us.

I love living in Bismarck now, and I'm actually happy we moved here. Like my dad told me, sometimes things we see as bad actually turn out to be good. So I'll end this by saying, "Thank you, God, for my family and friends and school, and please help Luke through his St. Bernard situation."